"It's Been A Long Time Since I've Been Interested In A Woman," Quade Said. "Yet The Instant I Saw You In My Bedroom…"

"You were interested?" Chantal's voice was barely a whisper.

"Oh, yeah. I can't tell you how many times I've replayed that first encounter. Those satin sheets sliding across the floor. You leaning over the bed. The creaking mattress."

"So…" Her gaze drifted to his lips, and it might have been his imagination, but she seemed to drift closer, too. When he breathed, his senses swam with her scent. "Where does that leave us?"

"Do you want there to be an us?" he asked.

"Do *you?*" she countered.

"I don't know," he said, smoothing his fingers down the length of her arm before he stepped away. "Hell, I can't even make up my mind if I like you or not."

Dear Reader,

Get your new year off to a sizzling start by reading six passionate, powerful and provocative new love stories from Silhouette Desire!

Don't miss the exciting launch of DYNASTIES: THE BARONES, the new 12-book continuity series about feuding Italian-American families caught in a web of danger, deceit and desire. Meet Nicholas, the eldest son of Boston's powerful Barone clan, and Gail, the down-to-earth nanny who wins his heart, in *The Playboy & Plain Jane* (#1483) by *USA TODAY* bestselling author Leanne Banks.

In *Beckett's Convenient Bride* (#1484), the final story in Dixie Browning's BECKETT'S FORTUNE miniseries, a detective offers the protection of his home—and loses his heart—to a waitress whose own home is torched after she witnesses a murder. And in *The Sheikh's Bidding* (#1485) by Kristi Gold, an Arabian prince pays dearly to win back his ex-lover and their son.

Reader favorite Sara Orwig completes her STALLION PASS miniseries with *The Rancher, the Baby & the Nanny* (#1486), featuring a daredevil cowboy and the shy miss he hires to care for his baby niece. In *Quade: The Irresistible One* (#1487) by Bronwyn Jameson, sparks fly when two lawyers exchange more than arguments. And great news for all you fans of Harlequin Historicals author Charlene Sands—she's now writing contemporary romances, as well, and debuts in Desire with *The Heart of a Cowboy* (#1488), a reunion romance that puts an ex-rodeo star at close quarters on a ranch with the pregnant widow he's loved silently for years.

Ring in this new year with all six brand-new love stories from Silhouette Desire....

Enjoy!

Joan Marlow Golan

Joan Marlow Golan
Senior Editor, Silhouette Desire

Please address questions and book requests to:
Silhouette Reader Service
U.S.: 3010 Walden Ave., P.O. Box 1325, Buffalo, NY 14269
Canadian: P.O. Box 609, Fort Erie, Ont. L2A 5X3

Quade: The Irresistible One
BRONWYN JAMESON

Published by Silhouette Books
America's Publisher of Contemporary Romance

SILHOUETTE BOOKS

ISBN 0-373-76487-1

QUADE: THE IRRESISTIBLE ONE

Copyright © 2003 by Bronwyn Turner

BRONWYN JAMESON

spent much of her childhood with her head buried in a book. As a teenager, she discovered romance novels, and it was only a matter of time before she turned her love of reading them into a love of writing them. Bronwyn shares an idyllic piece of the Australian farming heartland with her husband and three sons, a thousand sheep, a dozen horses, assorted wildlife and one kelpie. She still chooses to spend her limited downtime with a good book. Bronwyn loves to hear from readers. Write to her at bronwyn@bronwynjameson.com.

For Jen, my best writing buddy—
without your friendship and support and selflessness,
I might never have finished this story.

One

Cameron Quade wasn't surprised to see the sleek silver coupe parked in his driveway. Irritated, yes, resigned, yes, but not surprised. Even before he identified the status symbol badge on the car's hood, he'd figured it belonged to his aunt or uncle, one or the other. They probably owned a matched pair.

Who else knew of his impending arrival? Who else had just cause and reason for waving the Welcome Home banner? He'd been expecting Godfrey and Gillian to show up sooner or later but he'd have preferred later. Several years later seemed around about perfect.

As the front door clicked shut behind him, Quade let the weighty luggage slide from his fingers and a weightier sigh slide from his lips. His travel-weary gaze scanned the living area of the old homestead he'd grown up in, then narrowed on a wince.

The place had been unoccupied for twelve months

yet the gleam coming off every highly polished surface was damn near blinding. Someone had been busy but his aunt Gillian wielding a duster? If he could have summoned the necessary energy, he'd have laughed out loud.

As he wandered from room to room he did manage to summon a mild intrigue. The funky R & B tune piping from the stereo—a boy band?—didn't seem like Aunt G.'s taste, although the classic gray suit jacket looped over the hall stand did. As for the flowers—he traced a finger along the rim of a hothouse orchid—yeah, the artful arrangement on said hall stand reeked of her touch.

But the woman in Quade's bedroom, the woman in the classic gray skirt peeling back his bedclothes, was not his father's sister.

No way, no how.

"Come on, come on, pick up the phone!"

The woman's voice—low, smoky, impatient—drew his gaze away from the gray skirt and up to the cell phone clamped to her ear. She raked her other hand through her hair, one sweep from brow to crown that brought the thick dark mass into some sort of order. Temporary, he predicted, watching one curl bounce straight back up again.

"Julia. What *were* you thinking? Did I not specify *guy* sheets? Something practical, no frills?" She wrenched at the bedding, ripping it free from the mattress. "And you chose *black satin?*"

Practically hissing the last words, she flung the sheets behind her. They slithered across the highly polished floorboards to land just shy of where he stood, unnoticed, in the doorway.

"Good grief, Julia, you might as well have left a box of condoms on the pillow while you were at it!"

Quade's brows lifted halfway up his forehead. Black satin sheets and condoms? Not the usual homecoming gift, leastways not from his aunt and uncle. And he wasn't expecting welcome-home gifts from anyone else, especially this unknown Julia, the one copping an earful from the stranger in his bedroom.

"Call me when you get in, okay?"

Correction. *Whose answer machine* was copping an earful.

Equal parts amusement and bemusement curled Quade's lips as the discarded phone skidded across a side table and bumped to a halt against the wall. Still the same blue paint he recalled from his childhood. He'd wanted fire-engine red but his mother had stood firm. Luckily.

His nostalgic smile froze half-formed when the woman leaned across his bed. Holy hell. Quade tried not to stare, but he was only human. And male. And at his lowest point of resistance, completely lacking in willpower. Ten thousand miles of travel did that to a body.

Riveted, he watched her straight skirt ride up the backs of smoothly stockinged thighs. Watched the fine gray material stretch from classic to seam-threatening across a stunning rear end.

It was the first sight to snare Quade's total attention in those thousands of miles of travel.

Hiking her skirt higher, she slid one knee onto the mattress and stretched even farther, and he realized, belatedly, that she was remaking his bed. No, not his childhood bed but the big old double from the guest room—the antique one with the rusty springs. And as she leaned and bent and stretched and tucked, the mattress squeaked and creaked with a sound evocative of another kind of movement, a sound that stoked Quade's warm enjoyment of the scene to hot discomfort.

Hot discomfort as inappropriate as his continued silent observation, he decided with a wake-up-to-yourself shake of his head. He stepped out of the doorway and into the room and asked the first question that came to mind. "Why are you changing the sheets?"

She whipped around in a flurry of fast-moving limbs that put her off the mattress and onto her feet in one second flat. Or, more accurately, onto one foot and one shoe in one second flat. Her other shoe had sailed free midflurry and now lay on its side, stranded halfway between the bed and the discarded sheets. She faced him with one hand splayed hard against her pink-sweatered chest, with her eyes round and startled.

Eyes, he noticed, almost as intensely dark as her hair. Both contrasted starkly with her pale complexion, although her softly rounded face was in perfect harmony with her body.

"I haven't the foggiest who Julia is or why she's been choosing my bed linen," he continued softly, toeing the heap of satin out of the way as he came further into the room, "but I have nothing against her taste."

Her gaze whipped to the phone and back again, and he knew that she knew exactly what he'd overheard, but she offered no explanation, no comment, other than an accusatory, "You're not supposed to be here for another hour. Why are you early?"

She looked annoyed, sounded put out, and there was something about the combination that seemed oddly familiar. Quade tried to place her as he dealt with her objection. "We had a decent tailwind across the Pacific and got into Sydney ahead of schedule. Plus I'd allowed for fog over the mountains but it was surprisingly clear for August. I made good time."

Her attention slid past him, toward the doorway. "You're alone?"

"Should I have brought someone?"

When she didn't reply he lifted a brow, waited.

"We didn't know if you were bringing your fiancée," she conceded. "We decided to play it safe."

Hence the double bed. Hence the black satin and condoms. At least that made some sort of sense, or it would have done if he still had a fiancée to share his bed. As for the rest...

"We?" he asked.

"Julia and I. Julia is my sister. She's been helping me out." Or not helping, if her disgusted glare at the abandoned sheets was any indication.

Again, he felt that inkling of familiarity. Nothing solid, but... Gaze fixed on her face, he came a little closer. "Now we have Julia sorted, that leaves you."

"You don't recognize me?"

"Should I?"

"I'm Chantal Goodwin." She lifted her chin as if daring him to disagree.

He almost did. Hell, he almost laughed out loud in startled disbelief. While at university Chantal Goodwin had clerked in the law firm where he'd worked. Hell, he all but got her the gig but he didn't recall *ever* seeing that spectacular rear end. He did, however, recall her being a spectacular *pain* in the rear end.

"It was a long time ago," she said stiffly. "I dare say I've changed a bit."

A bit? Now there was a classic understatement. "You had braces on your teeth."

"That's right."

"And you've rounded out some."

"Nice way of saying I've put on weight?"

"Nice way of saying you've improved with age."

She blinked as if unsure how to deal with the compliment, and he noticed her lashes, long and dark and natural. If she wore any makeup, he couldn't tell. And in the sudden stillness, the total silence, he realized that the music had stopped. And that a nice warm hum of interest stirred his blood.

"So, Chantal Goodwin," he said softly, "what are you doing in my bedroom?"

"I'm an associate in your uncle's law firm."

"Well, *that* explains you being in my bedroom."

She had the good grace to flush, prettily, he thought. "I also happen to live just across the way—"

"In the old Heaslip place?"

"Yes."

"So, you're making my bed as a neighborly gesture? Kind of a welcome-home gift?"

That pretty hint of color intensified as she shifted her weight from one foot to the other. When *the other* turned out to be the shoeless one, she listed badly to the left. Quade steadied her with a hand beneath her elbow, taking her weight and enjoying the notion that he'd thrown her off balance almost as much as he was enjoying her pink-sweatered, softly flushing, female-scented proximity.

Clearing her throat, she pointed beyond his right shoulder. "Before I fall flat on my face, would you mind fetching my shoe?"

Quade retrieved it; she thanked him with a smile. It was no more than a brief curve of her wide unpainted mouth but it softened her eyes. Not quite black, he noticed, but the deep opaque brown of coffee…without the cream. That was reserved for her skin, skin that looked as velvety smooth as those orchids in his hallway.

"As I was saying—" She paused to slip her foot into the shoe. "Godfrey and Gillian wanted your place habitable before you arrived and because I live so near, I was…I volunteered."

Ah. His uncle—her boss—had volunteered her for the job. The Chantal Goodwin he remembered would have just loved that! "You cleaned my house?"

"Actually I employed a cleaning service. But the linen's all packed away and I didn't like going through your father's things. That's why I asked Julia to buy the sheets."

"Does Julia work for Godfrey, too?"

"Good grief, no." She shook her head as if to clear it of that staggering notion. "I was running short on time so she was helping me."

"By buying sheets…?"

"Exactly. Anyway, these ones—" she indicated the sheets on the half-made bed behind her "—are mine and because I had to go fetch them, I'm running late."

"For?"

"Work. Clients. Appointments." With quick hands

she resumed her bed making. "Julia also shopped for groceries. I'm sure you'll find there's enough to get by on. I took the liberty of having your phone connected, and the power, of course."

Quade folded his arms and watched her tuck the plain white sheets into ruthless hospital corners. "Leave it," he said, feeling unaccountably irritated by her seamless switch to business mode.

She straightened. "Are you sure?"

"You think I can't make my own bed?"

Unexpectedly her mouth curved into a grin. "Well, yes, actually. I've never met a man yet who could make a bed worth sleeping in."

Her wry amusement lasted as long as it took their gazes to meet and hold, as long as it took for images of rustling sheets and naked skin and hot elevated breathing to singe the air between them.

"I—" She looked away, off toward the wide bay window and the wild gardens beyond, then drew a breath that hitched in the middle. "I have to go. I'm running so late."

She started to turn, on the verge of fleeing, Quade thought. With a hand on her shoulder, he stopped her and felt her still. He picked up her discarded phone and pressed it into her hand.

Slowly, finger by finger, he wrapped her hand around the instrument. No rings, he noted, with a disturbing jab of satisfaction, just neatly filed nails, unpolished, businesslike. But he felt them tremble, and she retrieved her hand quick smart and took a small step backward. A reluctant step, he knew. Chantal Goodwin didn't like stepping back from anything.

"One thing before you go." He waited for her to turn, to meet his gaze. "You've done a first-rate job here considering you're not a professional house-maid.''

An almost-smile touched her lips. ''Thank you...I think.''

''So, what's in it for you?''

''Like I told you, it was convenient for me to help out, living so near.''

''And this—'' he waved his hand expansively to indicate the whole buffed and sparkling house ''—has to be worth a whole truckload of brownie points.''

One dark brow arched expressively. ''You think?''

''Yeah, I think.''

''Then I'd best go see what I can negotiate.''

This time he let her go although he stood unmoving, listening to the sharp *click-clack* of her sensible heels all the way down the long hallway, around his dumped luggage, and out the front door. Not fleeing, but hurrying off to work, to collect those brownie points.

To further her career. He should have figured that one out without any clues.

Funny how he hadn't recognized her, although in fairness to himself, she hadn't merely changed, she had metamorphosed. Even funnier was the way he'd responded. Hell, he'd been practically flirting with her, circling and sniffing the air. And it wasn't even spring yet.

Scowling darkly, he put it down to sleep deprivation and the complex mix of emotions associated with his homecoming. Combine that with the unexpectedness of finding her in his bedroom, leaning over his bed, and no wonder he'd forgotten himself for a minute or ten.

The next time they met he'd be better prepared.

*   *   *

Chantal didn't slow down until a passing highway patrol officer flashed his headlights in warning, but even after she eased her pressure on the accelerator her heart and blood and mind kept racing—not because of her near brush with a speeding fine, but because of her brush with Cameron Quade.

With time weren't teenage crushes supposed to fade? In this case, obviously not. Right now she felt as warm and flustered as when she'd first met the object of her teenage infatuation. He had fascinated her for years before that, what with all the retold stories—from her parents via Godfrey and Gillian—of his glorious achievements at the posh boarding school he'd been sent to after his mother died, then at law school, and finally his appointment to a top international law firm.

He'd done everything she aspired to, and everything her parents expected of her. Oh, yes, she'd heard a lot about Cameron Quade even before she met him, and she'd worshiped from afar. Up close he was worth all of the worshiping. Her skin grew even warmer remembering the moment when she'd turned and found him in that doorway. The perfect bone structure, the strongly chiseled mouth, the brooding green eyes and thickly tousled hair.

So long and lean and hard. So unknowingly sexy, so irresistibly male. So exactly how a man should look.

Chantal tugged at the neckline of her sweater and blew out a long breath as she recalled the way he'd looked right back at her. Like she was there in his bedroom for another purpose entirely. What was that all about?

Back in the Barker Cowan days he'd never looked at her with anything but annoyance or dismissal or—on one painfully embarrassing occasion that even now caused her to wince—with blood-freezing disdain.

And didn't he have a fiancée back in Dallas or Denver or wherever he'd been living the past six years? Kristin, if memory served her correctly. He'd brought her home for his father's funeral and she'd looked exactly like the kind of woman Cameron Quade *would* choose as a mate. Tall, stunning, self-assured—the direct antithesis of untall, unstunning, self-dubious Chantal.

She must have misinterpreted that look. Perhaps he'd been even more exhausted than he looked. After all, he hadn't even recognized her. As for Chantal herself…well, her wits had been completely blown away by his sudden appearance. Not to mention what he'd overheard.

Good grief, Julia, you might as well have left a box of condoms on the pillow while you were at it!

Had she laughed it off or explained that she usually didn't go around tossing phones at walls? Oh, no. She'd just stood there staring at him like some tongue-tied teenager…some *lopsided* tongue-tied teenager.

In her mind's eye she saw one low-heeled black court shoe spiral through the air in stark slow-motion replay. She groaned out loud.

Way to make an impression, Ms. Calm Efficient Lawyer!

Especially when making an impression was the whole point of the exercise. Godfrey had asked her to help him out, to check that the cleaners did their job and maybe stock the fridge, but she'd wanted Merindee prepared within an inch of perfection.

To impress the boss's nephew, to impress her boss.

She'd intended to be finished and long gone before said nephew arrived, but then she hadn't counted on the whole bed and sheets debacle...for which Julia had to wear some culpability, she decided, frowning darkly at her cell phone. She punched Last Number Redial and waited nine rings—she counted them—for her sister to pick up.

"Hello?" Julia sounded breathless.

"Were you outside? You better not have run—"

"Relax, sis. You know I'm beyond running anywhere."

In the background Chantal heard a deeper voice, followed by a muffled shush. Her frown deepened. "Shouldn't Zane be at work?"

"Oh, he has been." Julia sounded suspiciously smug. "We're working on our honeymoon plans."

Chantal rolled her eyes. "Good grief. You're six months pregnant. Shouldn't you be working on your nursery?"

Julia laughed, as she did so often these days. "It's been finished for weeks. Where are you, by the way?"

"On my way to work." In fact, she was just passing the Welcome sign at the eastern edge of the Cliffton city limits. "And, thanks to you, I'm running way late."

"Thanks to *me?*"

"You didn't hear the message I left earlier?"

"Sorry, we've been busy." Julia laughed huskily

then added in cavalier fashion, "Well, whatever the prob, I'm sure you'll deal with it."

"The *prob* is those black sheets you bought."

"Oh, no, they're midnight-blue. They *look* black but in the light they have this deep blue shimmer. Very classy but sexy, too, don't you think?"

Chantal didn't think about sexy sheets, at least not consciously. Before Zane Julia hadn't, either, and Chantal was still adjusting to this new mouthy version of her formerly meek and mild sister.

"Now, about tonight..." Julia shifted to a more businesslike tone. "Would you be able to collect the party platters seeing as you're in Cliffton?"

"Well, actually, about tonight—"

"Uh-uh, no way! You are my only sister *and* half of my bridesmaids and you *will* be at my shower."

"I was only going to say I may be running a little late."

"Oh. Then I'll have Tina bring the supplies. But don't be too late and don't forget it's costume."

How could she forget? The other bridesmaid, Zane's sister Kree, had taken complete control of the wedding shower arrangements because, in her words, Chantal's party skills needed serious surgery. A matter of opinion, Chantal sniffed. Some people preferred her quietly elegant dinner parties.

"You won't forget?" her sister prompted.

"No," Chantal said on a heavy sigh. "But I liked this relationship much better when *I* was bossing *you* around."

Julia laughed again then asked, her voice laced with suspicion, "What are you coming as?"

"A lawyer."

Julia groaned and Chantal smiled. "Before I go I should thank you."

"For?"

"Doing that shopping job for me. Sheets aside, you were a big help."

"Don't thank me, just give the man my business card." Chantal closed her eyes for a second and wondered if she could put the card under Quade's door. Or in his mailbox. "Oh, and you might toss in a personal recommendation. If this Cameron Quade saw your garden, he'd know I do good work."

"Look, sis, he may not want to do anything with the old place. He might not be staying."

"You didn't ask Godfrey?"

"I asked but I don't think he knows any more than I do about his nephew's plans."

"Easily fixed. What's the man's E.T.A.?"

Chantal shifted uneasily in her seat. For some inexplicable reason she didn't want to share news of the Cameron Quade encounter with her sister, at least not until she'd come to grips with it herself. "Today some time."

"So, when you pop over to welcome him to the neighborhood, you ask how long he's staying."

Chantal's response fell halfway between a snort and a laugh. *When you pop over.* Huh!

"What? I thought asking questions was what you lawyers did for a living."

"You watch too much television," Chantal replied dryly. Far more of her time was spent on reading and researching and documentation than in courtrooms. She cast a quick glance at the box of files on her passenger seat and felt her heart quicken. Some day soon she hoped that would change, and that the brownie points she'd earned this week would speed the process along.

"So, you'll see him over the weekend?" Julia persisted.

"You don't think this garden design thing could wait, say, until *after* your wedding?"

"No way! I need something to do other than worry about what we'll do if it rains."

"You did have to choose a garden wedding," Chantal pointed out.

"Yeah, yeah, I know. I chose a garden wedding and I chose to wait until spring so my guests would have something to look at other than bare-limbed trees."

"Like your belly?" Chantal teased, and was rewarded with her sister's laughter. Better.

They said their *see you tonights* and disconnected as Chantal braked at the first of three traffic lights in Cliffton's main street. The way her day was going, she'd likely catch every red. Her CD player flipped to the next disc and she remembered the one she'd left in Quade's house. Wonderful. As if she needed another reason to call on her new neighbor…

When you pop over, you ask.

If only Julia knew the half of it!

This morning she hadn't asked any of the questions that needed asking, and she wasn't talking about Julia's garden design aspirations. She was talking questions that had been gnawing away in her mind like a demented woodworm ever since she first heard of Quade's imminent return.

Questions such as, *What's a hotshot corporate attorney like you doing back in the Australian bush?*

And, *Has Godfrey asked you to join his firm?*

Questions whose answers might impact on her own career aspirations. Straightening her shoulders, she reminded herself that she was no longer a gauche teenager with no people skills. She was a mature twenty-five-year-old professional who had worked hard on her inadequacies, on overcoming her fear of not measuring up, at focusing on what she *was* good at, namely, her job.

As such, there was only one option.

Tomorrow she *would* pop over to Merindee and ask her questions.

Two

Two minutes later Chantal swung into the car park behind Mitchell Ainsfield Butt's offices and—thank you, God—found a vacant spot. Maybe her day was about to get better, although she wasn't betting any real money on it.

Juggling keys and phone in one hand, she jammed her briefcase under the other arm and balanced the box of files on one hip. With the other she nudged her car door shut—one of the few instances when a sturdy pair of hips proved an asset, she noted as she crab-walked her load between the closely parked cars.

The back door to the office block swung open just as she reached the stoop. And yes, her luck did seem to have changed for the better. The man holding the door for her, the man taking the box and briefcase and carrying them into her office was Godfrey Butt himself.

"Quite a load," he said, sliding it all onto her desk.

"The Warner files. Since I spoke with Emily I've been doing some further research—"

"Good, good."

Chantal bristled at the interruption, but didn't have a chance to object before he continued.

"And that other little job? Merindee all ready for Cameron's arrival, I trust?"

"Yes, absolutely." She forced herself to smile. "I called in this morning to drop off food and flowers."

"Flowers, eh? Nice touch. I'm sure Cameron appreciates your efforts."

Chantal wasn't so sure but who was she to quibble when Godfrey looked so pleased? Wasn't this *exactly* why she'd worked so hard on that dang house? "Do you have a few minutes, sir? Because I would really like to talk to you about Emily Warner's concerns."

"I was about to go out. Is this urgent?"

"It's important."

"What time frame—today, next week, this month?"

"The last," Chantal conceded reluctantly. "But I would appreciate your input sooner."

"See Lynda about finding some time next week." He was almost at the door before he paused, lips pursed consideringly. "Do you play, Chantal?"

Caught midway through a mental happy dance, his question caught her unprepared. Did she play...what? Then he started to swing his arms in a mock golf shot and the light dawned. Friday. Of course, the partners' regular golf date with People Who Mattered.

As Godfrey completed his follow-through, as Chantal considered the implications of his seemingly casual question, her heart kicked hard against her ribs.

Visions of green fairways and time-consuming strolls and relaxed back-slapping bonhomie with Partners Who Mattered popped into her mind.

"I haven't played in a while," she supplied slowly. How far should she bend the truth? "My game is probably a tad…rusty."

"Take some lessons. The new pro at the Country Club worked marvels with Doc Lucas's swing. When you're up to par, you can join us for a round."

"That would be…" She struggled to find the right description. *Perfect? What I've been waiting for? Terrifying? All of the above?* She swallowed. "Thank you, sir."

After the door closed behind him, Chantal spent several minutes riding a dizzying emotional seesaw. One second she wanted to punch the air with elation, the next she wanted to thwack her head—hard—against the desk. Because Godfrey's invitation came with a proviso.

Once her game was up to scratch.

Once she could be relied upon to spend some time on those verdant fairways of her imagination, instead of watching ball after ball leap into the water trap like lemmings into the sea. That's precisely what had happened the last time she'd attempted the "game." She deliberately inserted quotation marks because the word "game" connoted fun, and there'd been no fun in learning golf under her big brother's tutelage.

"But Mitch lacked the necessary teaching skills," she reminded herself, standing and pushing her chair aside. She never could debate worth a fig sitting down. "Not to mention how he rushed me and bullied me and laughed at my ineptitude. How could anyone learn under such conditions? With a decent teacher and the right motivation, I can learn how to hit that stupid ball.''

Same way she learned everything else. Preparation and practice and patience. With that personal credo, nothing had yet defeated her.

What about sex? a tiny voice whispered.

No contest, she argued. Inadequate preparation, insufficient practice, impatient tutor.

Sinking back into her chair, she reached for the phone and phone book. With receiver clasped between ear and shoulder, she flipped pages, dialed, then opened her schedule. She combed a hand through her hair, grimaced at the overgrown mess, but deleted Make Haircut Appointment. Ruthlessly she X'ed another six items on her To Do list—including Shop For Skirts One Size Bigger—and substituted Golf Lessons, all the while ignoring the nervous palpitations in her stomach.

Sure she hated golf, but she would push that little white ball from hole to hole with her nose if it helped raise her profile at Mitchell Ainsfield Butt, if it helped her earn enough respect to represent clients like Emily Warner. It wasn't that her current work was boring, more like…routine, when what she really craved was a stimulating challenge.

''Cliffton Country Club Pro Shop. May I help you?''

''I hope so,'' Chantal replied briskly. ''I need lessons and lots of them. How soon can I start?''

Twenty-four hours later Chantal was peering through the window closest to Cameron Quade's front door into a still, silent, seemingly empty house. The lack of response to her first dozen raps could simply mean he slept soundly. But, dear God, she did not want him opening the door straight from his bed. Possibly half-dressed, probably bare-chested, definitely ruffled.

Apprehension shivered up her spine…at least she figured it might be apprehension, or indecision, or, God help her, cowardice. Rubbing her hands up and down her arms, she turned and took six steps across the porch before halting her hasty retreat. Retreat? Cowardice? From the nebulous threat of a bare-chested man? No way, José. Last night she had braved a Kree O'Sullivan hosted bridal shower. A bare-chested man should be a walk in the park after that fracas.

The breath she puffed out formed a white vapor cloud of warmth as it met the chill morning air, but with renewed determination she strode back to the door and gave the brass knocker all she had. She figured the strident metallic clanking would carry all the way down to her house, three paddocks away.

Even if he were in the farthest of the sheds out back, he couldn't *not* hear it…could he?

The seconds ticked by. She tapped her foot—in the schmick two-tone golfing shoes purchased three years ago and worn, like the rest of her outfit, a handful of times. Tapping aside, the only other noise she detected was the scuffling of feral chickens in the undergrowth. She turned back to peer through the window one last time, pressing her face right up to the pane in a vain attempt to see around the corner…

"Looking for someone?"

She swung around too quickly. That was the only explanation for her sudden breathlessness, that and the enveloping sense of guilt at being caught in classic Peeping Tom mode. Caught, needless to say, by the very Tom she had hoped to catch a peep of.

He wasn't bare-chested, she noted irrelevantly. He hadn't just left his bed…not unless he slept in a snug-fitting olive polo knit with jeans worn near white in some interesting places. Not unless he was a very vigorous sleeper. For a film of perspiration dampened his brow, and as he came up the two shallow steps onto the porch she felt the heat of recent exertion radiating from his body.

One dark brow lifted, asking a silent question. Or prompting her to answer the one already asked, the one she couldn't quite recall with him standing so close, filling the air around her with body heat.

Looking for someone?

Yes, that's what he'd asked, in that smooth low voice that did strange things to her breathing. She waved a hand behind her, toward the front door. "I tried the knocker and when you didn't answer—" She shrugged. "I had decided you mustn't be home. Or that you were down the back in one of the sheds. Or taking a walk."

"You could tell all that by looking through that little bitty window?"

Wonderful. Now he'd not only caught her snooping, but he'd made her feel like a fool. Straightening defensively, she forced herself to meet his eyes. This morning they looked exceedingly green, as if they'd absorbed the color of the garden at his back. "I could tell by the lack of response. I rang long and loud enough to wake the neighbors."

Mentally she rolled her eyes. *She* was the only neighbor and she'd been awake for hours.

"I heard," he said dryly. "I was around the back, chopping wood."

Which explained the sleeves carelessly shoved up to his elbows and the way his top clung in places, as if to sweat-dampened skin. She cleared her throat, averted her eyes, tried to concentrate on something else. Like the fact he was chopping wood. Dang. She hadn't considered firewood. "I didn't think you'd bother with the log fire."

"And if you *had* thought I'd bother?"

"I would have had a load of split wood delivered."

"Then I'm glad you didn't think of it."

He moved away to lean against one of the pergola's timber uprights. This is good, she told herself, trying not to notice the pull of denim across long muscular thighs and the dark dusting of hair on his bared forearms. Trying to ignore the little jump of response low in her belly.

Concentrate, Chantal. From this distance you can enjoy a nice neighborly conversation and extract the necessary information without it sounding like an interrogation.

"Why are you glad I didn't have firewood delivered?" she asked.

"I enjoyed the exercise."

His gaze rolled over her, taking in her daffodil-yellow sweater complete with crossed-golf-clubs logo, her smart tartan A-line skirt, her thick stockings (it was winter, after all), and the shoes she loved to death. He crossed his arms over his chest—not bare but impressive nonetheless. "Looks like you've got the same thing in mind."

It was her turn to lift her brows in question.

"Exercise," he supplied.

"Yes. I have a golf…" She stopped herself admitting to a lesson. "A game of golf this morning."

He made a noncommittal sound that could have meant anything. Then he shifted slightly and the sunlight streaming between the overhead beams caught his hair, burnishing the ordinary brown with rich hues of chestnut and gold.

Of course he didn't have ordinary brown hair—how could she have even thought it? Inadvertently her fingers tightened…around Julia's business card in her left hand. "My sister, Julia—"

"The bedroom decorator?"

"Actually, she's a garden designer. An absolutely brilliant gard—"

"Was she responsible for the flowers?" he interrupted again.

"No. I brought the flowers."

"And the food?"

Inhaling deeply, she fought her simmering irritation. "Julia brought the food and the first round of sheets. I brought everything else—"

"Except the firewood."

For crying out loud, did the man have a license to exasperate? First he had to turn up looking so…so distractingly male, and then, just when she'd composed herself, he had to interrupt every second sentence.

Chantal impelled herself to breathe in, breathe out, before continuing in a reasonable, patient tone. "Julia adores redesigning old gardens and would love to draw you up a design, if you're interested. If you're staying that long."

A coolness came over his expression. "So, the real

reason for your visit is to find out how long I'm staying."

"I can't say we're not curious because the whole town is agog—"

"And are you visiting on behalf of The Plenty Agog or to satisfy a more personal curiosity?"

Chantal lifted her chin. "I promised to pass on Julia's message about the garden."

"Come on, Chantal. You didn't come here to talk garden design. What is it you want to know?"

"Why do you think I have an ulterior purpose?"

"You're a lawyer."

Affronted, she stiffened her spine. "And you are?"

"An ex-lawyer."

Ex? Chantal moistened her suddenly dry mouth. "So you haven't come home to join Godfrey's practice?"

"Hell, no." He shook his head as if the idea were ludicrous. "Scared I was after your job?"

"I just like to know where I stand," she replied stiffly. And on a more personal level? Yes, she was curious. Yes, she had to ask. "What *are* you going to do?"

"Short-term, as little as possible. Definitely nothing that aggravates me. Long-term, I haven't made up my mind."

"About staying here?"

"About anything."

Chantal's curiosity grabbed a tighter hold. "And your fiancée...?"

"I don't have a fiancée." Expression tightly shuttered, he looked toward her car. "Haven't you a golf game to get to?"

She wanted to stand her ground, she *ached* to stand

her ground, to ask the rest of the questions hammering away in her brain, but he took her elbow firmly and turned her toward the driveway. She had the distinct impression that digging in her heels would have led to a forcible and undignified removal. As it was she had to scramble to keep up with his rangy strides.

"Nice car," he said, opening the door of her brand-new Merc. "A country lawyer must do better than I thought."

Partway into the car, she stilled. It wasn't so much the words as his cynical tone. "You have something against country lawyers?"

"Not if they leave me alone."

He said it mildly but that didn't prevent barbs of irritation blooming under her skin. Before she could form a cutting comment about *this* country lawyer's work prettying up his house, he surprised her by saying, "I didn't picture you ending up back here working for Godfrey."

For a second she was speechless. She hadn't imagined Quade picturing her at all. "How *did* you picture me?" she asked slowly.

"Corporate shark. You still got that bite, Chantal, or did you lose it along with the braces?"

Chantal bared her teeth and he surprised her by laughing. Right there, up close, with only the car door separating them, she felt the effect zing all the way into her bones. Wow.

Still smiling—how could she have forgotten those dimples?—he tapped his watch face. "Don't want to miss tee off."

She lowered herself into the driver's seat and scrambled to regather her wits. No way was she driving off without saying all she'd come to say. "If your heart is set on minimum aggravation, you need help with this gard—''

''I can handle my garden.'' He closed the door.

She opened her window. ''It's going to take more than sweat and muscle to get this mess in order.''

''I said I can handle it.''

He projected such an aura of confidence and competence, Chantal didn't doubt it. He would chop his own wood and fix his own garden and in between times he would probably round up all the renegade poultry and start an egg farm. Which didn't mean that *she* wouldn't have the last word in this particular debate.

Kicking over the engine, she tossed him a trust-me-I-know-what-I'm-talking-about look. ''Julia does wonderful work. If you want evidence, come down and take a look at my garden sometime.''

Without a backward glance she spun her car in a tight circle and headed down the driveway, wondering why the heck that last line had sounded like *come up and see me sometime.* When delighted laughter bubbled from her mouth she reprimanded herself severely.

You should be feeling ticked off, Chantal, not turned on. That crack about country lawyers was completely uncalled for. And although you asked your questions, his answers weren't exactly expansive. Doing nothing won't keep a sharp mind like his happy for long, and what then? Do you really think Godfrey won't ply him with offers that would tempt a saint? And Cameron Quade has never been accused of being a saint.

But despite her self-cautioning, despite the fact that Julia's card remained clutched in her hand and she'd again forgotten all about her CD in his player, she found herself turning up the volume of her car stereo and humming along. However the words buzzing around in her brain were very much her own.

She had got the last word in.

She had made him laugh.

He didn't have a fiancée.

Hands on hips and eyes narrowed against the brightening morning sun, Quade watched her drive away. It was only then that he realized he was smiling—smiling in response to that last exchange, in response to her determination to win the last word. She was quite a competitor, Ms. Chantal Goodwin. That much hadn't changed.

The smile died on his lips, gone as quick as a blink of her big brown eyes. If he could expunge the residual buzz of sexual awareness from his body as easily, he'd be a happy man. No, a satisfied man, he amended. The word "happy" hadn't fit his sorry hide in…hell, he didn't even know how many years.

Immersed in the take-no-prisoners race up the corporate climbing wall, he hadn't noticed his priorities turning upside down. He hadn't noticed the lack of enjoyment and he had ignored the lack of ethics. Happy hadn't even figured. It had taken a soul-shattering event to open his eyes, to send him flying home to Merindee. True happiness—the kind you didn't have to think about, the kind that was just there, as natural as breathing—seemed intertwined with his memories of this place, back before his mother succumbed to cancer and his broken father lost all his zest for life.

Twenty years.

Quade scrubbed a hand across his face, then cast his gaze across the rolling green landscape. He had no clue how to pull his life back together only that this was the place to do it. He hadn't lied about his plans. He did intend doing whatever he felt like, day to day, hour by hour. He was going to live in jeans and unbuttoned collars, and sample as much wine as he could haul up from his father's cellar. Who knows, he might even start sleeping upward of four hours a night.

Away in the distance, where the Cliffton road climbed a long steep incline, a silver flash caught his eye. Chantal Goodwin on her way to golf and he just bet it wasn't a hit and giggle weekend jaunt with her girlfriends.

Oh, no, Ms. Associate Lawyer would have an agenda on the golf course same as she'd had an agenda fixing his house and visiting this morning. She hadn't come to tote business for her sister's garden business. Worry about her career had sent her snooping for information.

To find out if *he* was after *her* job.

A short ironic laugh escaped the tight line of his mouth. He didn't doubt that Godfrey would make overtures. He expected it. But uncle or not, benefactor or not, he had no qualms about turning him down. Some time in the future he might feel like putting on a suit and tie and going back to work. But not to the law. Long-term he intended staying clear of all things pertaining to his former profession.

Especially the women.

Three

There she went again. Bobbing up and down and scurrying back and forth like a squirrel gathering stocks for the winter. What was she up to?

Distracted by the distant figure, Quade lifted a hand to swipe at his sweaty forehead but a blackberry thorn had snagged his sleeve. Ripping his arm free, he pushed to his feet and let out a long whistle of frustration. After three hours of hacking and pulling and chopping and cursing, he'd had it with this weed. There had to be an easier way.

Hands on hips, he squinted out across the paddocks to where Ms. You're-Going-To-Need-Help popped in and out of view. He would as soon flay himself with one of these briar switches than admit it to her face, but she was right.

After she'd driven away the previous morning, he'd taken a hard look at the jungle that used to be his

mother's pride and joy, and immediately gone searching for tools. But for all the inroads he'd made, there
were sections he didn't know how to tackle. And—
he glared pointedly at the blackberry outcrop—sections he wished he could take to with a bulldozer. He
needed help in the form of expert advice. If said
expert happened to be driving said bulldozer, he
wouldn't complain…although he couldn't imagine
Chantal Goodwin's satin-loving sister at the controls
of heavy machinery.

While he enjoyed the fantasy elements of that mental image, Quade watched and waited, but the bright
red of his neighbor's sweater didn't reappear. He
wasn't surprised. She'd been following the same pattern ever since he first spotted her shortly after lunch.
Suddenly she would appear out of the thicket of trees
that cloaked the western side of her house, a bright
dab of color and motion ducking about on a lush
green backdrop, then she would disappear back behind the trees.

What the hell was she up to?

One thing for sure and certain, standing here peering into the lengthening afternoon shadows was providing no clues. Hadn't she invited him down there
to inspect her sister's handiwork? And hadn't the
small matter of not thanking her for her efforts preparing his house been nagging at his conscience ever
since yesterday morning? He could almost see his
mother shaking her head reproachfully.

*Didn't I teach you better manners than that, Cam-
eron?*

Determined to make amends, he hurdled the back
fence and set off across the paddocks.

* * *

The thicket of trees he'd been studying on and off all afternoon proved to be a windbreak protecting a good-size orchard, and that's where he found her. There at the end of a soldierly row of bare-branched trees with a golf stick clutched in her hands and a look of such intense concentration on her face that she neither saw nor heard nor sensed his approach.

Dressed in the same cute little skirt as yesterday morning, she stepped up to the first in a line of balls and adopted the stance. After swiveling her hips in a way that caused Quade's mouth to turn dry, she started into her backswing. With his gaze fixed hip height, he saw her lower body lock up and wasn't surprised when she lost the ball way off to the right.

She rolled her shoulders, stiffened her spine and moved on to the next ball. One after another she sent them spraying all over the closely mown pasture that fronted her house.

Suddenly her squirrel-like behavior made sense. She'd been scurrying about collecting golf balls, bringing them back, then hitting them all out there again. Time after time after time. He'd witnessed that same dedication firsthand working alongside her, but golf was supposed to be a game of relaxation. And this *was* Sunday afternoon.

After the last ball rebounded off a tree trunk at least forty degrees off-line, her shoulders dropped again.

"Do I take it yesterday's game didn't go well?" he asked.

Near black with startled indignation, her gaze swung his way. "How long have you been standing there?"

"Long enough."

"Well, there you go." She laughed, but it was a

short, sharp, humorless sound. "You're a firsthand witness to my disproving an old adage. Practice does not always make perfect."

"Ever heard the one about not reinforcing bad habits through practicing them?"

"What bad habits?" she asked warily.

"You're locking up in the lower body. You need to keep loose, relaxed."

Eyes narrowed and faintly indignant, she watched him approach. "You were watching my lower body?"

"Guilty. But in my defense, you are wearing that skirt." Quade allowed himself a pleasurably slow inspection of *that* skirt, before lifting his gaze to meet hers. She did that surprised blinking thing he'd noticed before, the one that made him think she wasn't used to handling flattery. Strange from a woman with her looks.

Then she straightened her shoulders and looked him right in the eye. "So, Quade. I'm sure you didn't come down here to critique my golf swing. What is it you want to know?"

Quoting his words right back at him…how like a lawyer! He almost smiled and it struck him that ever since he walked into her orchard he'd been enjoying himself. A discomforting notion, given the company. "After you left yesterday it struck me that I hadn't thanked you for the effort you put into my house. I know it's belated but thank you."

"You walked down here to say thank you?"

"And to repay you for the cleaning service and shopping."

"Godfrey took care of the accounts."

Quade's lips tightened. This wasn't good enough.

Not the way she deflected his thanks or the way she dismissed his attempt to recompense her. "Fine," he said shortly. "But I do owe you for the time and the inconvenience."

"That's not nec—"

"How about a quick golf lesson?" He rode right over the top of whatever objection she'd been about to make. "We can work on your lower body."

A faint, rosy flush tinged her throat as her gaze fell away from his. Hell. He hadn't meant that kind of work but now *his* lower body responded. "I do mean golf."

"Of course." She lifted her chin. "How do I know that you know what you're doing?"

"Good question."

Did he know what he was doing? Did he really want to tempt himself with hands-on-Chantal-Goodwin lessons? In anything?

But when her expression narrowed with skepticism he took the seven-iron from her hand, grabbed a handful of balls from the pail by her feet and tossed them to the ground. After a couple of idle swings to limber up, he hit one with a macho swagger he'd forgotten he possessed. It felt good.

"Easy as that," he concluded as they both watched the ball soar into the next paddock.

"You're a man. You hit long without even trying."

"Sure, length's important." And he *was* talking about golf, despite the way her gaze flicked down his body. Despite the way his…length…felt compelled to answer for itself. "But it's not the only consideration. Accuracy is crucial."

He illustrated by turning around and knocking the

next ball smack down the center of the gap between two rows of fruit trees.

"You do realize you're going to have to fetch those balls you're hitting all over the countryside."

"Later, but first you're going to hit a few yourself."

He offered her the iron, but she didn't take it. Annoyed by her hesitancy—and, hell, couldn't she have at least acknowledged the sweetness of that last shot?—he folded her unyielding fingers around the handle. They remained stiff, so he wrapped his hands over hers, molding them into a grip. Soft hands, he noticed, with a sinking feeling in his gut. Exactly as he'd feared.

"What have you done to your hands?" she asked, her question hitching a little in the middle.

Quade followed the direction of her gaze, down to where his large hands completely overlapped hers on the iron. For a moment he could only think of that, her soft warm hands under his, wrapped firmly around the hard shaft...

"Your hands?" she repeated.

Dragging his mind up out of the gutter, he noticed the raw scratches. He'd forgotten about the thorns. Standing this close, with erotic imagery pumping through his body, he could be excused for not remembering his name.

"I've been gardening," he said shortly.

"I thought you intended doing nothing aggravating."

"I intended doing whatever I felt like. Today I felt like gardening."

"Gardening or attacking blackberries with your

bare hands?'' She drew a breath, then let it go. "Have you put anything on those wounds?''

"Such as?''

"Antiseptic. Salve. Peroxide. I don't know what you're supposed to use.'' Her voice rose sharply, aggrieved, and when he looked into her eyes he noticed they echoed her distress. Something stirred deep in Quade's gut, something that wasn't lust.

Something that scared the bejeebers out of him.

He let her hands go and took a quick step backward. Away. "I guess that means you're not going to play nurse,'' he teased, desperate to lighten the mood.

But the words acquired a sensual weight of their own and hung there between them as her gaze roamed his hands, his forearms, his abdomen. Color rose from her neck to taint her cheeks, and he knew she was thinking about tending his wounds, about touching him in all those places.

This time the heat in Quade's gut *was* lust, pure, simple and so intense it held him paralyzed while he imagined the soft hot caress of her hands on his skin.

She lifted her face to look right at him. Standing this close he could see the black rim of her coffee-dark irises, could feel the allure of their rich depths. Eyes a man could sink right into, he thought, if a man wanted to lose himself. There had been times these past months when Quade had wanted to lose himself, badly, but never to another woman whose only passion was career.

"I'm not much good at playing anything,'' she said finally, and her voice held a husky edge that stroked every place her roaming gaze had missed. "Nurse, sports, golf.''

Smiling at her wry quip, he took another mental

step backward, although his libido lagged behind. "And your golf swing needs a lot more attention than my scratches. Come on, Chantal." He gestured from the iron in her hands to the golf ball at her feet. "Show me what you've got."

"You want me to just hit it?"

"Yup. Relax and slog it."

"What about the accuracy you mentioned as crucial? What about caressing the ball?"

Quade lifted a brow. "Who's been telling you about caressing the ball?"

"Craig." The admission came slowly, reluctantly. "The local pro."

"Huh." So that's why she was all decked out by Golfers R Us. To impress Craig, the ball-caressing pro. Feeling unaccountably snippy, he watched her go through the same shoulder-rolling attempt at relaxation he'd witnessed earlier. Her white-knuckled grip indicated a distinct lack of success. "Didn't your Craig mention two hands as one?"

"He's not *my* Craig." Adjusting her grip, she stepped up to the ball. "And I usually get that bit right."

Quade stopped her with a hand on her shoulder. Through the plush warmth of her sweater he felt her tension ratchet up a notch and had to stop himself kneading the tightness. "Just relax, no pressure. We'll start without the ball. Transfer your weight," he instructed quietly.

"Like this?"

"Not bad." With a sense of fatalism riding him hard, he moved close behind her, puffed out a breath. Okay, he could do this. Adjust her hands without allowing his to linger. Guide her arms without wrapping his around her waist. Steady the sway of her hips without drawing them snug into the cradle of his. "Can you feel the difference?"

"All I can feel is you breathing on my neck," she murmured in that sense-stroking voice.

Quade closed his eyes for a moment. He decided not to tell her he'd been thinking about putting his mouth on her neck, right there on the delicate pale skin behind her ear.

"How was that?" she asked, finishing off her swing.

"Better, but follow right through."

He kept her at it, correcting, adjusting, suggesting, encouraging. Trying not to admire her determination, trying not to admire anything about her.

"The trick is having your weight in the right spot when you connect with the ball."

Dark gaze hot with frustration, she swung around to face him. "When *do* I get to connect with the ball?"

"When you stop lifting your head."

"Craig said my head position is just fine."

"Craig was probably too busy watching your ass to pay any attention to your head."

Outraged, her eyes widened along with her mouth. He didn't give her a chance to speak. He placed a hand at the back of her neck and directed her head into the correct position.

"Head down, like this, when you strike the ball." The tension in her neck vibrated into his hand. The heat of her skin hummed into his blood. He moved his palm, just a fraction, massaging gently. "You're not relaxing."

With an angry exclamation she swung away from him. "How can I relax with you touching me?"

Holding his hands out, palms up in a conciliatory gesture, he retreated several yards. "Hey, I'm not feeling too relaxed, either, not with that club aimed in my direction."

She lowered the iron she'd been brandishing like a weapon and sighed. "I'm sorry. It's been a long day."

"You're right. But before we pack it in, how about you give that swing one last try?"

She looked dubious.

"I'll stand way over here. No breathing. No instructions." He gestured toward the ball. "Have at it."

When she connected with a solid thunk, when it sailed out in an almost straight trajectory, he could see the delight in her face. In her smile. Felt it shining as brightly as the late-afternoon sunshine, reaching out to wrap him in its warmth. What could he do but smile right back?

"There you go," he said through his smile.

"No need to sound so smug." She swung the club around in several rapid-fire circles, like a gunslinger after a showdown. "I was hitting an occasional decent one before you happened along."

"You were woeful."

"Was not."

Quade laughed out loud—at her belligerence and because he simply felt like it—and when she closed the distance between them and stood smiling up at him, he felt a powerful urge to capture that delight between his hands, to taste it on his lips. When he felt her gaze focus on his mouth, he knew he'd been staring at the source of his temptation.

That full-lipped, soft-textured, smart-talking mouth.

Sobering instantly, Chantal stared up at him. "Thank you."

"My pleasure," he replied with equal gravity.

As she absorbed the shift in mood, everything inside her stilled. He was looking at her as if it *had* been a pleasure, as if he'd enjoyed standing close enough to breathe on her neck, as if he wanted to kiss her.

Now. On the lips.

A wave of longing washed through her, blindsiding her with its intensity, urging her to move closer, to place her hands on the broad wall of his chest. His heart pounded reassuringly loud so she slid her hands higher, up toward his neck.

She moistened her lips. Her lids drifted shut.

Suddenly hard fingers circled her wrists, forcibly removing her hands, setting her firmly back on her feet. When Chantal opened her eyes he was already striding out across the pasture, bending to pick up a golf ball, then moving on. Dang. No, this situation deserved a much harsher word than that old crock. Damn.

Damn, damn, damn, damn, damn.

She'd been a whisper away from his lips, from his kiss. And she had no doubt that Cameron Quade would kiss with the same confidence, the same sure-handed skill, as he'd employed when tutoring her golf swing. Missing out on a kiss like that was enough to make a woman weep, especially a woman who'd never been kissed by a true craftsman. With a heavy sigh, she picked up her pail and stomped off after him.

Had she read him wrong? She didn't think so, although perhaps she'd moved too fast. How fast *was* too fast? Some men didn't like aggressive women…although her lame attempt at a kiss hardly fit that tag. And that girlfriend he'd had at Barker Cowan, that Gina Whatsername in Contracts, she hadn't possessed a passive bone in her long, tightly strung body.

Perhaps she should have grabbed hold of his sweater. Or his face or his hair. Lord knows, she wanted to bury her fingers in that thick dark head of hair. Whatever, her prekissing technique obviously needed as much work as her golf game. Perhaps she should enquire if the local community college ran any classes along those lines. Seduction for Beginners. Or Bedroom Technique 101.

The questions, the answers, the conjecture looped through her brain in gloomily escalating circles the whole time she looped the front pasture, clearing it of golf balls. By the time they met by the side gate into her garden the sun was kissing the horizon with its last rays of light. He dropped a handful of balls into her pail, his expression cool.

"Thanks again," she murmured. "For helping me out with the lower body thing."

"You'll do fine once you learn to relax."

Nodding, she swallowed audibly. Any second now he'd take that big step backward, lift a hand in farewell and saunter off home. The thought filled her with an unreasonable panic. She wanted a chance to make up for her kissing gaffe. She wanted to make him laugh again.

"The way I hit that last ball, I feel I owe you more than a casual thanks." She moistened her dry mouth. "Would you like to stay for supper?"

"Can you cook?" he asked.

"I took lessons."

"And I should be reassured? You told me you took golf lessons, too."

"I haven't poisoned anyone." She paused for effect. And because she couldn't help smiling at his dry answer. "At least not recently."

For several heartbeats she thought he wouldn't respond to her crack, but just as the disappointment sank heavily into the pit of her stomach, he smiled. Full dimples and all. As the impact of that smile danced through her blood, her heart burst into a rumba.

"So tell me, Chantal... Lessons in golf, lessons in cooking. Do you do anything by instinct?"

"I would say no, except I just invited you to supper and I think that might qualify." Her voice sounded low and husky, not at all as light as she'd hoped. "Will you stay if I promise to relax and keep it loose?"

He didn't answer right off and in the tricky twilight his expression was unfathomable. The moment stretched, as taut as the tendons in her fingers where they clutched the pail. Perhaps she should let go the air backing up in her lungs. Perhaps she should laugh and ease the moment. Perhaps she should...

"I don't think that's a good idea," he said quietly.

"Oh." She swallowed a huge lump of disappointment. "Any particular reason?"

"Here's the way I see it—I gave you a golf lesson because I owed you. Then you invited me to supper because you figured you owed me. Next, I'll be asking you out to dinner because I owe you for the supper.'' He paused long enough for her to imagine candlelight and violins, knees brushing under the table, hands touching and retreating across a snowy white cloth. "Where do you suppose all these favors will end?''

Heart thumping, she moistened her lips and thought about his antique bed all dressed up in satin that shimmered under the midnight moon.

"Better to call us even here and now, don't you think?''

Didn't she think? What *had* she been thinking? If Cameron Quade wanted to start a relationship, there would be women queuing up all the way to Cliffton for the privilege. If he wanted someone sliding between his satin sheets, he would find a woman who knew how to slide, instinctively, not a woman who needed lessons in the basics of male-female relationships.

"Before I go, there is one more thing," he continued smoothly. "You said Julia designed your garden."

Chantal perked up slightly. "I did and she did. Do you want to look around? I just happen to have her card in my pocket."

She extracted the card and handed it over. He pocketed it without a glance. "How about doing the guided tour tomorrow? It's getting a bit dark now."

"I won't be home any earlier than this, unfortunately."

"Working late?''

"Golf lesson." She pulled a face.

"No drama. I'll have Julia show me some of her other work."

"I'd reschedule if I could, but Craig's already put himself out to fit me in."

"I'm sure he has." A cynical smile twisted his lips as he turned to leave. "See you around, Chantal."

What did he mean by that? *I'm sure he has.* Said in *that* tone of voice? Was he implying... She lifted her voice enough to carry across the orchard. "Craig has no interest in me other than the fact that I'm paying him to teach me golf."

"If you say so."

"And he does not watch my ass."

He turned, hands on hips, and she could still see that smile, white in the gathering darkness. "Then *he's* an ass."

Four

Doing as little as possible wasn't all it was cracked up to be. Quade arrived at this conclusion six days later, as he prowled around his sodden grounds. His hands itched to grab hold of a shovel or a hoe or a pair of tree loppers, but Julia Goodwin's instructions had been clear.

"Hands off until I say otherwise."

When he objected she'd asked if he really wanted her help or not. He'd unclenched his teeth and agreed to meet with her Saturday afternoon, which, she'd apologetically informed him, was the soonest she could get out there.

"Transportation difficulties," she'd said. "Plus the forecasts are for a wet week."

A less honest man might have blamed his subsequent restlessness on the waiting. Or on the week's unrelenting rain. Or the hollow emptiness of a house he remembered resonating with laughter and redolent with the smell of home cooking.

All of the above could claim some culpability but, in truth, his mood owed as much to self-flagellation for turning down Chantal's invitation. He couldn't cook worth a damn, he couldn't order home delivery out here in the boonies, and he'd turned down a home-cooked meal.

That made him even more of an ass than the short-sighted golf pro.

The long wet week provided plenty of opportunity to appreciate how much he had enjoyed her company—she'd amused him, stimulated him, and irritated him all at once. Yet when she issued that invitation, when she mentioned loosening up and he started to sink into the sultry depths of her eyes, he'd felt a compelling need to get out while he still could. As if she posed some kind of danger.

As if.

Sure, there was something appealing about her combination of soft curves and sharp tongue, something erotically enticing about her silken skin and rich eyes. But Chantal Goodwin was no beauty, not in the big scheme of things. Resisting the attraction was as simple as recalling the single-mindedness of career women with their sights set on the top, as easy as remembering the callousness of Kristin's deceit.

He had called Chantal. She'd not been home. A busy lawyer like her had places to be, hours to bill. That cynical thought kept his feet planted on his side of the fence and a scowl planted on his face, and the latter felt much more at home than the smiles she'd coaxed out of him.

Better to concentrate on whipping his garden into

shape, he decided, not to mention the land beyond, which had fallen into an equal state of neglect. He didn't picture himself as Farmer Jones but he could employ a consultant, same as he was doing to compensate for his lack of gardening knowledge.

The heavy throb of a large engine brought him out of his scowling reverie just as a big black tow truck appeared in his driveway.

Julia Goodwin drove a tow truck?

Quade did a mental double take as the vehicle lumbered to a halt, partly obscured by shrubbery. Expectancy tightened his gut at the sound of a door squeaking open then thudding shut and didn't relent when a woman strode into sight.

She was a slightly taller, even curvier, more stunning version of her sister. Her thousand-watt smile looked capable of lighting every corner of his enormous cellar. And despite all that, Quade's pulse remained slow and steady. If *this* Goodwin sister invited him to supper, he would accept in a heartbeat.

"Cameron Quade, I presume? I'm Julia Goodwin, which you've probably figured out all by yourself."

Smiling back, he offered his hand. "Just Quade."

"Just Quade, huh?" She took his hand and shook it firmly. No tremor, no spark, no heat cascading through his system. Odd, given his extravagant reaction to her sister…but fortunate, given the big sternfaced man who'd followed her from the truck and who now placed a proprietary hand on her shoulder.

"Zane O'Sullivan." He extended his hand over Julia's other shoulder.

"In two weeks' time he gets to be my husband," Julia added.

"Lucky man." Quade met the big guy's gaze,

which happened to be as strong and testing as his grip.

"I think so."

"You *know* so," Julia corrected, turning on her heel in a quick three-sixty appraisal of her surroundings. The action caused her unbuttoned coat to swing open and when she came to a halt with her hands planted on her hips, the tightness returned to Quade's gut with viselike intensity.

Julia Goodwin was visibly, round-bellied pregnant.

Struggling to pull himself together, he forced his gaze up, away, anywhere but *there*. Hell, she wasn't the first pregnant woman he'd seen, not even in the past month, since he'd found out about Kristin. About the pregnancy he'd known nothing about; the pregnancy she had chosen to terminate.

"When are you due?" he asked slowly, and his voice came out strained, as if strangled by the tightness spreading into his chest and up to his throat.

"Early November."

"Is that a problem?" O'Sullivan looked as confrontational as his question sounded. Quade didn't blame him—not when another man had been gawking at his fiancée's belly. It's a wonder he wasn't wearing Zane O'Sullivan's substantial fist in the center of his face.

Quade forced his lips into some semblance of a smile. "No problem. A surprise, that's all."

"Well, hey, it was a surprise this end, too, but of the very best kind. This little one—" Julia patted her middle. "—doesn't stop me doing much. I wish I could say the same for Daddy."

She tempered the cheerful complaint by resting her hand on O'Sullivan's arm and smiling up at him. A four-year relationship and Quade couldn't remember a time when Kristin had looked at him in quite that way. Hell, in the last year she'd barely found time to talk about anything outside of work, and she'd had her own agenda for keeping that channel of communication open.

"I told Zane I'm not doing any of the physical work," Julia continued, "but perhaps you can reassure him? You know, on the digging and lifting front?"

Snapping free of his bitter memories, Quade fixed the other man with a direct look. "I'm only in the market for design and consultancy. I *want* to do all the digging and lifting."

O'Sullivan considered him levelly for a long moment before nodding. "Fair enough."

Satisfied, Quade shifted his attention back to Julia. "You didn't mention the wedding. You're going to be busy."

"Not with Chantal on the team."

"Everything's organized?"

"With the precision of an army maneuver," Julia replied. "And I appreciate something to do other than worrying about the weather."

Quade gestured at the overgrown beds. "You think this will be enough to keep you busy?"

"Piece of cake. Speaking of which, I don't suppose you have any of that chocolate cake left?"

Clueless, he looked to O'Sullivan for help, and received a don't-ask-me-mate shrug.

"I felt sure there was a Sara Lee in the shopping I did for you, but not to worry." Hand on belly, Julia grinned ruefully. "It's probably best if I don't spoil my appetite, seeing as Chantal's cooking dinner."

"She's a good cook?" Quade couldn't help asking.

"She's good at everything she sets her mind to."

"Except golf."

He hadn't meant to share that observation, but it appeared he had. A stunned silence followed.

"Chantal has taken up golf?" Julia asked on a rising note of disbelief.

He hitched a shoulder. "She's taking lessons."

"From Craig McLeod at the Country Club?"

"Pretty Boy's a golf pro?" O'Sullivan sounded as surprised by this as Julia was about the Chantal/golf connection.

While the other two discussed their former schoolmate, Quade chewed over the nickname. He wasn't sure if he should be laughing or scowling. He didn't want to ask, but he couldn't help himself. "People call him Pretty Boy?"

"Not to his face."

"Which, I hasten to add, really lives up to the promise," Julia chipped in. "How is it you know about Chantal's golf lessons?"

Her question interrupted a mental scenario where Chantal's backswing caught McLeod square in his pretty face. The image cheered Quade far more than it had any right to. "She mentioned it, in passing."

"In passing, huh? Do you two pass often?"

"We're neighbors."

It might have been his imagination, but her everpresent smile seemed to turn speculative. "So, Just Quade, before we get down to garden business, what plans do *you* have for dinner tonight?"

"Hey, sis. Where are you?" Piping from the answering machine, Julia's voice sounded even chirpier than usual, Chantal decided, although that might have only been in comparison to her own unchirpy mood. ''I thought you'd be slaving over a hot stove with us coming to dinner in less than an hour. Which is why I rang. Hope you don't mind but we're bringing your neighbor…although that took some talking. You must have made quite an impression. Not. Anyway, see you soon.''

Chantal sank slowly into a lounge chair. Quade was coming to dinner. Exactly as she'd imagined in all those midnight fantasies. Except—unlike her fantasies—he wouldn't be turning up on her doorstep with a bottle of wine in one arm and a bunch of flowers in the other.

Oh, no, he was being dragged by the bootlaces because Julia had a way with persuasion. With a growl of frustrated despair, Chantal buried her face in her hands. She would kill Julia, truly she would, but first she needed to pull herself together. She peered through a gap in her fingers and groaned. On second thought, she would postpone pulling herself together until she had pulled her house together.

Scooting around the living room, she straightened furniture and tossed pillows onto chairs, arranged the magazines into careful piles and gathered up all her work files from the floor in front of the fire. The dead fire. Cold ashes. Unwelcoming. *Help!*

With a hand splayed against her chest, she could feel her escalating heartbeat. A glance to the mirror above the hearth—hair a windswept mess, no makeup, unflattering brown sweater—did nothing to alleviate her rising panic. She had forty minutes. She needed a plan of action. She needed music, a soothing antidote in times of stress.

Six long strides took her to the sound system and she dropped to her knees. Brows knit, she ran a finger down the CD tower. Where was her favorite stress-buster? Her mind slid instantly to the last time she had needed it...

It was likely *still* sitting in Quade's stereo.

The forty minutes flew, but not as fast as Chantal's hands or feet. In the time between first hearing the rumble of Zane's approaching truck and the sound of Julia calling, "We've let ourselves in, okay?" she changed into her best jeans and her second-favorite rust-colored knit.

Her favorite off-white angora lay inside out on the bed, discarded on an issue of practicality. Pasta sauce would be so much less noticeable sloshed down the front of *this* sweater, and, when she cooked, stuff inevitably ended up sloshed. She constrained her hair with a couple of tortoiseshell clips, dusted her overheated face with powder, then, with significant effort, stopped herself dashing back at the same breakneck speed.

Difficult, but she impressed herself by managing.

Unfortunately she didn't manage to coax her face into a smile. As she walked—*slow down, Chantal, don't stride!*—into the large informal living room, she felt as if her attempt might actually crack her cheeks. When she noticed Quade, alone, bending down to a low bookcase shelf, she gave up her attempt altogether.

Side-lit by a table lamp, he looked—she licked her lips and blew out a hot breath—he looked delicious. She knew the kelly-green sweater would do amazing things to his eyes and when he hunkered lower, his jeans pulled tight and did amazing things to his thighs and buttocks. Oh, my Lord!

Pulse leaping as crazily as the flames in the fireplace, she watched him select her well-worn copy of *To Kill a Mockingbird* then straighten. "How old were you when you first read this?" he asked, still with his back to her.

How had he known she was there? Could he hear the pounding of her heart above the music? Chantal swallowed and prayed her voice would work. "I don't recall. Fourteen, maybe." A little husky, but working, which impressed her all over again.

"And you decided you wanted to be a lawyer?"

"I was never going to be anything else," she said simply.

He turned the book over in his hands, touching the cover in a way that caused her skin to tingle. As if those strong hands stroked her with the same gentle reverence. "I bet there's a big difference between what you're doing now and your childhood dreams," he said, turning to face her. "I bet you dreamed of being a big trial lawyer."

"Didn't we all?"

"Not me. I never did acquire the gift of rhetoric."

"I don't know about that." She arced a brow at him. "Although your particular gift might see you in constant contempt."

"You think I curse too much?"

Tilting her head on the side, she smiled wryly. "Let's just say you've always been a straight-shooter."

"Are you referring to that...difference of opinion...we had at Barker Cowan?"

Difference of opinion? What an interesting interpretation. "As I recall, it was more a hauling over the coals."

"You deserved it."

Chantal felt herself stiffen reflexively. "I was perfectly justified—"

"See? A difference of opinion, just as I called it."

Chin raised combatively, she glared into his green eyes and saw he was fighting a smile. Dang. How could she retain her righteous indignation with that smile hovering, teasing, threatening to turn her to instant mush?

"Water under the bridge," she said with a dismissive shrug, but only because he'd managed to totally deflect her argument. She still knew she was right, she just couldn't remember why. "Where did Julia get to?"

"She went to see if she could help in the kitchen."

"And Zane?"

"He followed."

"What on earth could they be doing all this time?" She frowned crossly, and then her brain kicked in again. "Oh."

His smile spread. "Indeed."

They were probably lip-locked at this very moment. She wanted to roll her eyes and say something smart, but with her gaze fixed on the curve of Quade's mouth all she could think was *lucky, lucky Julia.*

"I brought something—"

"My CD?" Distracted by kissing-envy, she jumped in without thinking, and he stared back at her blankly. Okay, not the CD... "My sheets?"

"I didn't know you'd left a CD and as for your sheets—" He looked right into her eyes. "They're still on my bed."

This was exactly why she'd sent Julia shopping for new sheets. To keep his hot body—his hot *naked* body—from between hers. Chantal swallowed weakly. "I thought you preferred the satin ones."

"Yeah, but yours turned out to be much softer than I imagined."

"High thread count."

"If you say so." His shrug highlighted the breadth of his shoulders. She imagined them bare, in golden-skinned contrast to her stark white linen, and her knees turned to putty. "Don't you want to know what I did bring?"

He inclined his head toward the coffee table and for the first time she noticed the two bottles sitting there.

"Do you like merlot?" he asked in a voice as intoxicating as that soft red brew. But before she could reply, Julia's head appeared through the doorway to the kitchen. She looked flushed and very thoroughly kissed.

"There you are, sis. Do you want me to do anything to help with dinner? Because I'm starving."

Chantal gathered herself. She had guests, a dinner to prepare. A bedazzled head to clear. "You can*not* eat the food before it's served. That would be helpful."

Julia grinned, then popped something into her mouth. It looked awfully like the remains of one of the dinner rolls. "Oops, too late."

The only way she could concentrate on cooking was to chase all chattering you-didn't-mention-what-a-first-grade-hunk-Quade-is distractions from her kitchen with instructions to set the table. Delving deep into the chest freezer for more bread rolls, she sensed a new disruption.

Her first abstracted thought was: *so that's how he knew when I came into the living room—he felt me eyeballing his backside.*

Her second abstracted thought: *if I stay here much longer, generating this amount of body heat, I'll defrost the whole freezer-load of food.*

While she extracted herself from the freezer depths, she rued the fact that her jeans, like everything else in her wardrobe, fit a little too snugly.

"Julia sent me after a corkscrew."

"Top drawer, beside the stove," she instructed.

He fetched it—she heard the drawer slide open then click shut—but she felt the touch of his gaze as she placed the rolls in the microwave. Suddenly her roomy kitchen felt very small, the lack of words between them awkward.

"For some reason I'm one roll short," she said, punching buttons to start the oven. She turned to find him leaning against the bench top, tapping the corkscrew against his thigh. A frown drew his dark brows together.

"Sorry for the lack of notice. Julia said you wouldn't mind."

"Julia's right—I don't mind. And the bread shortage isn't because you're one extra but because *she's* been sampling the goods."

She crossed to the stove, lifted the lid and carefully stirred the simmering soup. It looked good, smelled even better. Thank you, God.

"Knowing Julia," she continued conversationally, "you'd have had little choice on whether you came or not."

"I had choice. That bossy thing you Goodwin girls have going doesn't sway me."

Funny, but she'd never heard *bossy* sound like a compliment before. It was *that* voice, *that* mouth. Irresistible. The word drifted unbidden through her senses but she shook it away. "So, why did you come?"

"Curiosity."

What a curious answer… She turned a little, resting her hip against the stove, so she could see his face. "Curiosity about?"

"Your sister says you're an excellent cook."

And he didn't believe her. Well! Indignation rising, she lifted a ladle full of the thick orange puree and tilted it this way and that in the light.

"Pumpkin?" he asked.

"Roasted pumpkin with green apple and thyme."

"Gourmet," he murmured but she noticed him inhale the aromatic steam. She noticed his eyes haze just a smidge and her stomach dipped with satisfaction. He would change his mind about her cooking skills before the night was over.

"Would you like a taste?" she asked.

"Is it safe?"

Perhaps it was her imagination, but his cool Midori gaze seemed to slide to her mouth and back again. Chantal felt the impact flow through her blood in a prolonged wave of longing.

The touch of his lips wouldn't be safe, not to her sanity, not to her senses, but she didn't care. Oh, how she didn't care!

Gaze locked with hers, he slowly ducked his head to the ladle suspended between them. When he sipped from the edge of the tilted spoon, she felt her own lips open reflexively, felt her tongue touch the very center of her top lip. Felt a soft sigh of appreciation slide between her open lips. Saw something flicker darkly in his eyes. Desire? Resolve?

He leaned closer, beyond the spoon, and another sound escaped her throat, a sound of heightened anticipation. When his tongue touched her top lip, one soft stroke, she allowed her lids to drift shut. She needed to concentrate, to categorize each nuance, the whisper of his exhalation against her cheek, the slight change in angle that brought their lips into perfect alignment, the sensual slide of his tongue. Top lip, bottom lip. Sweet, spicy, hot. So delicious, the rush of flavor, of heat, of desire, but still just a sample, she knew, of what was to come...

Her knees turned weak, her shoulders slumped, her elbows gave way as a rich multitude of sensations coursed through her body. And then the ladle slipped from her fingers, bumped down the front of her jumper and clattered to the floor. Eyes flying open, she jumped back just as Julia barreled through the door. Pulling up short, she took in the scene in one raised-eyebrows look, turned on her heel, and left as quickly as she'd arrived.

Which left Chantal to deal with sloshed soup and one very uncomfortable man. He stood rubbing his forehead and looking as if he couldn't quite believe what he'd just done. *She* couldn't quite believe what he'd just done. She definitely couldn't believe what he was about to do...

He grabbed a dishcloth and started dabbing at her sweater. Down her abdomen, over her belly...and everywhere he touched seared like molten flame. Face flushed, pulse galloping, she drew in a shallow shuddery breath and felt him still. His eyes were lowered but she saw his nostrils flare and a shiver—hot, cold, *yes, please*—raced through her.

But he pushed the cloth into her hand and muttered, "That's got the worst of it," before stepping well clear.

Disappointment thundered hard on the heels of hope. Obviously he didn't want to talk about the kiss, let alone carry on where they'd left off.

Well, fine. She wasn't about to ask. Or beg.

"I guess I'd better get on with this cooking or we won't be eating till midnight," she said, shucking off a disturbingly intense sense of regret. She ducked down to grab a saucepan, dashed to the sink, back to the stove.

"Are you all right?" he asked after a frantic minute's activity.

"I'm fine. Why?"

"You look a bit…flustered."

Really? she thought. *Only flustered?* She could have sworn she looked somewhere between full boil and complete meltdown whereas he looked as cool as ever. Totally unaffected. Her heart did a duck and dive.

"Heat from the cooking." She flapped a hand in front of her face and inspiration struck. "Or perhaps I'm coming down with something. I've been feeling a bit fluish all day."

"You have?"

Well, no, but when he frowned at her she thought he looked concerned. Concerned she was contagious, no doubt, so she kept on talking. "The other day we were playing the back nine and got caught in the rain. By the time we made it to shelter, we were drenched.''

''Golf in the rain? Isn't that a bit much even for you?''

Chantal bridled at his tone of voice. ''The shower caught us by surprise.''

''The clouds gave you no clue?''

''I didn't care about the clouds,'' she snapped back. ''I needed to catch up on my lessons.''

''With Craig I presume?''

''Yes.''

He snorted. Then said nothing while she measured pasta and counted to ten to control her temper. She about had it under control when he muttered, as if through a tightly clenched jaw, ''It's only a game, Chantal.''

''You think I put myself through all this frustration for *a game?*'' she asked, whirling around to stare at him.

''Let me guess…golf is a smart career move. You want to impress Godfrey and maybe a client or two?''

Yes, she had taken it on for precisely that reason but it had become a personal challenge, a task to conquer. She wanted to succeed. But she wasn't about to make any apologies or to defend herself. She merely murmured, with just a touch of sarcasm, ''How perceptive of you.''

''Not particularly.'' His tone was as cutting as his gaze. ''Kristin would play golf in a hurricane for a pat on the head from her boss.''

He left her standing there stunned, not by his words but by the bitterness that sharpened the taut planes of his face and glittered in his eyes. By the knowledge that whatever had broken up his engagement had totally torn him up inside.

Five

"**O**h, no, you don't." Julia moved pretty speedily for a well-fed pregnant lady, snagging Chantal's arm before she could follow Quade and Zane and a cartload of crockery into the kitchen. "Yes, they're men, but I think we can trust them to pack a dishwasher."

"They're my guests."

"Technically I'd say more freeloaders than guests. Besides, Quade offered."

"He was being polite. No one offers to do dishes because they want to."

"True, but in this case you're doing them a favor."

Incredulous, Chantal laughed.

"No, really. They've been dying to get rid of us womenfolk so they can talk cars to their hearts' content." Julia tugged at Chantal's sleeve. "Let's go take a weight off. And please, could you try to relax?"

After Cameron Quade had raised her core temperature to boiling with one expert kiss, only to dunk her straight into the ice-cold water of his condemnation? No, she didn't think she could relax any more now than she had during dinner. Not when she kept recalling the look in his eyes when he mentioned Kristin's name. Not when her own response was a worrisome need to reach out, to soothe the hurt, to make it better. She was pretty sure Cameron Quade wasn't looking to her for emotional healing.

Finally she relented to her sister's insistent arm-jiggling and allowed herself to be led to the lounge setting by the fire. She didn't follow Julia's eloquent suggestion to take a weight off.

"If you're not going to sit, could you at least stop pacing?" Julia said after several seconds. "I'm getting tired watching you."

Chantal planted her feet in front of the hearth, forcing herself to still. Unfortunately this allowed her sister to fix her with a now-I-have-you-alone look. *Way safer to instigate the conversation myself,* Chantal decided. "What do you mean about the men wanting to talk cars?"

"Apparently Quade has some old sports classic in his shed." A smug smile curved Julia's lips. "Zane says its line and shape are almost as sweet as mine."

"The MG," Chantal said softly, recalling the car's sexy low-slung frame as clearly as if she'd seen it yesterday.

"The what?"

"The old sports car—it's an MG."

Julia shook her head. "You amaze me. How did you know that?"

"I…" Chantal hesitated. Why not share the whole sordid tale? It would definitely distract Julia from the story she really wanted to hear, the one about what she'd stumbled upon in the kitchen earlier. "Do you remember the summer I clerked at Barker Cowan? The firm Quade used to work for?"

"I remember how deadly important it was for you to clerk at the 'right' places. I remember *those* discussions around the dinner table," Julia said dryly.

"Well, it *was* important."

She'd wanted to experience a diversity of practices and to learn from the best in their fields, although in this case there'd been another factor influencing her choice. A twenty-something-year-old hunk of a factor.

She couldn't stand still; she had to pace. "It was the October long weekend. I was home from uni and I heard Quade was visiting with his father, so I drove out there. I wanted to know more about the firm, to see if I wanted to clerk there." A perfectly acceptable reason, she had decided at the time, to meet the intriguing Cameron Quade. "Anyway, his father answered the door and said Cameron was down at the shed, tinkering with the car."

"Ahh. So he was working on this MG way back then?"

Yes and no. Chantal moistened her dry mouth and decided to spill it all. "When I walked in, it wasn't the car he was working on."

Julia's brows rose sharply. "Who was he, um, working on?"

"An associate at Barker Cowan, as it turned out. Quade's father hadn't mentioned he had company, although I was so naive I'd probably still have waltzed right in there."

Almost seven years and she still flinched recalling

that moment of discovery. Still felt the rapid flush of heat that had washed through her, part embarrassment and part fascination.

"They didn't see you, right?"

"Good God, no. I turned and ran." Although not straight away. In fact, she'd been too paralyzed to move for a long enthralled moment.

"How did you know it was an MG?"

Chantal stopped pacing and blew out a hot breath. "I'm observant. Besides, I was looking anywhere but at…them."

"I can't believe you never told me about this." Julia puffed out a disbelieving breath before continuing, "I can't believe you ended up going to work at this Barker place."

"Mother organized it through Godfrey. She thought she was doing me a favor."

And so began the summer-in-hell, as she struggled to shut out those car hood images and her own fantasies born of them. She'd dreamed of being the woman spread across stark red duco. In her dreams she had felt the cool steel under her back and the hot man against her front; she'd experienced the magic of a lover's kiss and heard the low sounds of pleasure in her own throat. From each such dream she'd woken perspiring, disoriented, and still untouched by any lover.

"Wow," Julia breathed softly, as if party to Chantal's secret thoughts. "How did you deal with seeing Quade and what's-her-name every day?"

"I focused on the work." *Or at least I tried to.*

"But could you look them in the face? You know, around the coffee machine or over depositions or whatever law clerks do?"

"You remember me at nineteen." Chantal's attempt at a smile felt leaden. "Take a wild guess."

"Hmm...even before you transformed yourself into Ms. Cool and Competent, even when you were a bookish nerd with no social skills, you never chose avoidance. In fact, under pressure you tended to go the other way." Eyes widening, she slapped a hand to her cheek. "Were you very obnoxious?"

"Insufferably."

"Argumentative?" Julia asked, grimacing as if she dreaded the answer.

"Naturally."

"Oh, dear." Shaking her head, Julia started to laugh and Chantal's own smile grew until it warmed her from the inside out. Oh, but it felt good to share something personal, painfully personal, and to end up laughing about it. Although now she had started it seemed like she had to tell the rest.

"There's more," she said, taking a sobering breath and feeling the warmth of shared laughter and memories begin to chill. "There was this...incident. To cut a long story short, I was trying to impress Quade by impressing his boss and it backfired."

"He wasn't impressed?"

"Understatement."

Julia winced sympathetically.

"I was perfectly justified, though. He had no right to dress me down as he did."

Julia's mouth twitched. "Goes without saying. And you know, this whole story explains a lot."

"About?"

"About why you're like you are with him."

Chantal felt her shoulders stiffen. "How am I?"

"Not yourself, that's for sure. I've never seen you

so frazzled, sis. Not since you came back here a fully-fledged lawyer, at any rate. During dinner you didn't sit still long enough—''

"I've had a lousy day, okay? The crowning glory being you dropping an extra dinner guest on me.''

"Lousy days have never driven you to drink before.''

"I often have a glass of wine with dinner,'' Chantal defended stubbornly. "You know that.''

"A glass, yes, but tonight you could have dispensed with the glass. It only slowed you down.''

"Very funny.'' Chantal pulled a face. She knew she'd only had two glasses—three at most. Because she'd needed to take an edge off her nervous reaction to Quade beside her at the table. His scent, the brush of his knee, the memory of his lips on hers, the pain in his eyes. The whole confusingly complex issue of her feelings for the man.

"Is it so obvious?'' she asked, stomach churning. Did she really want to know the answer?

"The fact that you like him?'' A telltale blush started to rise in Chantal's throat and her sister clapped her hands with delight. "You're blushing which means you *do* like him.''

Chantal rolled her eyes. "I'm not about to engage in a game of *do so, do not.*''

"You are definitely blushing.''

"It's the fire. Plus I've been feeling fluish all day. Not to mention all the hot air you're spurting.''

"Pish!'' Julia's delighted gaze narrowed slightly. "I've always wondered what kind of man it would take to light your fire.''

"I hardly know him.''

"And this matters, why?''

"He's…" Chantal paused to weigh her words.

"Hot?" Julia teased, wiggling her eyebrows. "Sexy?"

"Does Zane know you feel this way about another man?"

"It's not working, you won't distract me. He's…what?"

"He's not interested," Chantal supplied finally. *Yes, he's hot. Yes, he's sexy. Yes, he kissed me but then he wished it back.*

"How do you know? You're hardly an expert on men."

And wasn't that the truth! Heck, before her distant fascination for Quade matured into her first full-scale crush she'd never spared men a thought. But that summer had exposed a gaping hole in her education, a hole she'd spent the next several semesters at university attempting to fill. Interaction Between The Sexes turned out to be the only subject she ever failed.

"Well?" Julia prompted. "How do you know?"

"I asked him to supper…he wasn't interested."

"Perhaps he wasn't hungry."

"And perhaps he isn't interested. He wasn't exactly busting down doors to come here tonight, was he?"

Julia's expression turned contemplative. "Methinks he protested a little too much."

"Yeah, right," Chantal scoffed while something inside leaped to life.

"Hey, I've been watching you two dancing around each other all night. And I don't know what I interrupted in the kitchen earlier, but I know when I'm interrupting."

"You don't think it's completely one-sided? Oh, heck, what am I thinking?" She laughed, but it was a nervous uncertain sound in perfect harmony with everything churning inside her, with every self-doubt and insecurity. "What does it matter? I have no clue how to go about this, what to do, even if I want to—"

Julia leaned forward and touched her arm, stopping her midinsecurity. "Why is it you relish every challenge work throws your way but you completely wuss out when it comes to men?"

That stopped Chantal for a moment, but only for a moment. Then she answered truthfully. "There's no set procedure, no course I can study."

"Quade would be a master class."

Skillful hands and talented lips, patience and finesse...a premonition of how that class might play out shivered through Chantal. Julia must have seen the reaction and misinterpreted, because her expression softened sympathetically. "Scary, huh?"

"I am not sc—"

"Yeah, yeah, I know. You don't do scared, at least not out loud. You also tend to go after what you want."

"This is different. Quade's...difficult."

Julia's brows rose. "And you think a challenge should be easy?"

"Not easy, just doable. I like to think I have some chance of succeeding."

"It's always about success with you, isn't it?"

"Yes. Yes, it is." Chantal expelled a harsh laugh. "Heck, I spent all those years chasing after you and Mitch, trying to measure up, vying for some scrap of our parents' attention."

"There never was enough to go around, was there?"

"Once I realized how to win their affection...I guess it's become habit."

"Well, don't let it become a habit you can't kick." Her sister's tone grew serious, her gaze strong and steady. "You spend way too much time with your work."

"I love my work. It's the *only* thing I do well and the only place I feel competent, okay?"

"Pish! You do everything well. What about the cooking and the flower arranging and the—"

"I took courses and I practiced and I *made* myself do well. But with my work...it's not an effort. It *is* my fun, okay?" Eager to escape, Chantal rose to her feet. "I'm going to make coffee. Would you like anything?"

For a long moment Julia looked mulishly like she wouldn't be deterred, as if she would keep hammering away at her insecurities, attacking the comfort blanket of her work. But in the end she let it go, diverted by the prospect of after-dinner treats. "Do you have cake? Chocolate, preferably? You always have good stuff in your pantry."

"By that, I gather you mean *bad* stuff."

Julia waved that distinction aside derisively. "Your addiction to junk food is one of your few redeeming qualities. Don't spoil it."

It was a throwaway line, Chantal knew that. She shouldn't have needed to ask... "I have other redeeming features?"

"Well, sure. For a start, there's your complete lack of vanity. You have no idea how stunning you are. Or could be, if you tried a bit harder."

Chantal rolled her eyes.

"Then there's the most important one—you would do anything for your family. I know that. Mitch knows that."

She could have played coy, could have denied it, but Julia had that one right. "Thanks." It was all she could manage through the sudden cloying thickness in her throat.

"You're welcome. Now, how about that cake?"

Shaking her head, Chantal headed for the kitchen door, but a sudden thought brought her up short. "What we've just talked about—everything—could it be under the cone?"

"The cone of silence? Of course." Julia smiled, nostalgically, Chantal thought, as if remembering childhood confidences shared under their own version of *Get Smart*'s cone of silence. "We haven't done that in a long time, have we? Same as we haven't talked, really talked like this, in ages. Let's do it more often, okay?"

Chantal was too choked up to answer so she simply nodded.

"Oh, and one last thing…"

Hand poised on the kitchen door, Chantal waited.

"I figure it's past time you took on something—or someone—that really challenges you, even scares you more than a little. Something that really *is* fun." She held up a hand. "Don't say anything, just promise to think about it, okay?"

"More coffee?" Chantal asked.

Her husky-edged voice and the slow sweep of her dark-eyed gaze cranked Quade's awareness up another notch, but before he had a chance to adjust she was on her feet—*again*—in full hostess role. He felt his jaw clench.

With the dishes done and the coffee made, they had settled in front of the open fire which should have been all homey and relaxed—*would have* been all homey and relaxed—if the furniture pieces weren't so strictly aligned, if a few cushions and magazines were tossed on the floor and if Chantal herself would sit still and relax.

Covering his cup with one hand, he unclenched his jaw enough to speak. "Forget the coffee. Find yourself a comfortable spot, park that delectable rear end, and take the rest of the night off," he said, low enough so as not to reach the ears of Julia and Zane, who sat cozily on the lounge talking wedding plans.

She blinked, long black lashes against smooth pale skin, and then her gaze seemed to gravitate toward his lap. Quade's body was quick to respond. Shifting uncomfortably in one of her big leather easy chairs, he told himself the effect was subliminal. A man's reaction to a suggestive glance, he decided, watching a delicate flush stain her cheeks. He swore silently.

Every time he finished convincing himself how snugly she fit the tough career woman stereotype, every time he resolved to leave her to her Kristin-like ambitions, some piece of paradoxical behavior turned his thinking around. Those shy-girl flushes, her concern over his scratched hands, the self-derision over her golf game. Her tentative response to his kiss, as if she didn't quite know what came next.

Hell, he'd come back to Plenty to sort out his life not to complicate it. And from where he sat—from where his body surged just imagining those tight hip-hugging jeans sliding into his lap—Chantal Goodwin represented one king-size complication.

As for her family...his gaze swung to where the other two sat, still immersed in their own conversation. Sometime during the afternoon O'Sullivan had graduated to Zane and Julia had slipped right under his guard. He'd been after a helping hand with his garden not the hand of friendship.

Watching them together filled him with...hell, he didn't know what it was. Some complex mix of envy and anger and regret over what he no longer had, and a hollow sense of loss for what he could never regain. Resolutely, he shoved those thoughts aside. No more self-pity, no more self-castigation, he reminded himself. He had moved past that mawkishness, not to any place concrete but he was working on it. Huffing out a breath, he forced himself to zone into the conversation.

"Did I tell you Mother rang this morning, wanting to know if we've chosen a time for the rehearsal?" Julia's question was directed at Chantal who had chosen to park her delectable rear end on the floor instead of in the vacant chair, or in his lap.

"Have you decided on a night?" she asked back.

Julia pulled a face. "I don't see why we need to practice at all."

"Easy for you to say," Zane muttered. "You're experienced."

"Best if everyone knows where they have to be, and when," Chantal added.

"Which is just fine if *everyone* could get to a rehearsal!"

"You'll have to ring Mitch and Gavin tomorrow, tie them both down to a definite answer."

Frowning, Quade backed the conversation up a few steps. "You've been married before?"

"Just the once," Julia answered cheerfully. "First time around I was looking for all the wrong things."

Same here. Except he was thinking about his career, about how he'd chosen law for the money and the prestige, and how Kristin had chosen him for the very same reasons. All the wrong reasons. A muscle jumped in his tight jaw, and he felt the touch of Chantal's gaze.

"Perhaps we could talk about something other than weddings," she suggested. To protect his sensibilities? Did she think he needed cosseting?

"Marriage isn't a touchy subject with me," he said shortly.

"It is with Chantal," Julia supplied. "She has very strong opinions on the subject."

"And why wouldn't I? In my job I see too many couples who have vowed to love and cherish tear each other apart over divorce settlements."

She'd spoken evenly, almost with restraint, and Quade couldn't stop himself from playing devil's advocate. "That's the ugly side."

"It's the one I see."

"You don't have to look far to see the other side." His gaze flicked to the happy couple then back again.

"Yes, Julia's about the happiest woman this side of the Great Divide but that doesn't alter history. First time around, she was plain miserable." She glanced apologetically toward her sister before returning her attention to Quade. "And as for our brother Mitch, well, his marriage breakup is damned near killing him."

Quade kept his gaze locked on hers, on eyes that

glowed more fiercely than the flames at her back. Because she ached so deeply for her brother, because she felt so intensely for both her siblings. "And what about you, Chantal?" he asked. "Have you vowed to save yourself from all this heartache?"

"Let's just say marriage isn't on my To Do list," she replied with a cynical half smile. It froze almost immediately. "Oh my God, I didn't think..." She shook her head remorsefully. "I'm sorry."

"Why? Because it's not on my To Do list anymore?" And he showed her a true cynic's twisted smile. "No need to apologize. I've moved on."

An awkward pause followed, the silence broken only by the stark crackle of burning firewood, and then by Julia groaning about bladders not structured for two.

In a sudden rush of activity, Zane helped her to her feet, and everyone else followed suit. Julia dashed off to the bathroom, Chantal started gathering coffee cups, and Zane yawned widely. "Time to call it a night. I've got an early start tomorrow. I'll warm up the truck and get the heater going. Coming, man?"

Before he could answer, Chantal cleared her throat. "He'll be along in a minute," she told Zane.

Too surprised to object, he waited through their thank-yous and goodbyes, until Zane had let himself out the front door. Then he waited while she drew a deep breath and straightened her shoulders. He heard the clink of cups touching, as if she had clutched her load more tightly. From where he stood it seemed like she didn't particularly relish whatever she had to say.

"I'm truly sorry about before," she started softly. "I should have thought before I opened my mouth."

"Is that why you kept me here? Is that all you wanted to say?"

"No." She lifted her chin and looked right at him. "Why did you kiss me?"

Shaking his head, he expelled a short wry-sounding laugh. Of all the questions she could have asked, he hadn't expected that one. "Damned if I know."

His gaze slid back to hers, caught and held. The atmosphere seemed to do the same, to catch and hold and wait in tense anticipation for whatever came next. He decided it might as well be the truth, as much as he knew of it.

"I haven't looked sideways at another woman in four years, not when I was with Kristin, and not since."

She moistened her lips. "How long since you broke up?"

"Six months." He rubbed at his jaw. "Six months and I simply haven't been interested. Yet the instant I saw you in my bedroom..."

"You were interested?" Her voice was barely a whisper.

"Oh, yeah. I can't tell you how many times I've replayed that first encounter. Those satin sheets sliding across the floor. You leaning over the bed. The creaking mattress."

"So..." Her gaze drifted to his lips and it might have been his imagination but she seemed to drift closer, too. When he breathed, his senses swam with her scent. "Where does that leave us?"

Before he could do more than think *anywhere you'd like,* the bathroom door smacked shut. She jumped guiltily. A cup slipped from her grip and thudded to the carpet, and she immediately moved to retrieve it. He stayed her with a hand on her arm. The sound of footsteps signaled Julia's approach and Chantal's question still hung there, suspended in the charged atmosphere, unanswered.

"Do you want there to be an us?" he asked.

"Do *you?*" she countered.

"Ready to go?" Julia asked coming into the room. For the second time she stopped in her tracks, eyebrows raised as she looked from one to the other. Quade didn't care. When Chantal squirmed he tightened his hold, ignoring her soft hiss of disapproval. He waited until she stilled, until she looked back up at him, eyes spitting her annoyance. And he realized he had no clue how to answer her question.

"I don't know," he said, easing his grip on her arm. He smoothed his fingers down the length of her delicate angora sleeve, so at odds with the fiercely held tension in the arm beneath, then stepped away. "Hell, I can't even make up my mind if I like you or not."

Six

At lunchtime the next day, Chantal admitted defeat. She simply couldn't focus on the papers spread before her on the dining-room table, a fact that confounded, annoyed and frustrated her in equal measures.

This was the Warner case, for Pete's sake, an estate wrangle with as many complicated twists and as much high drama as any soap opera...plus a wronged step-daughter who just happened to be a scrappy fighter. Most days Chantal couldn't find enough hours to spend building Emily Warner's case. It represented everything she loved most about her job.

Today wasn't "most days."

For a start it was the day after Cameron Quade showed her ten seconds of pure lip-to-lip bliss. It was also the day after he'd told her he wasn't sure if he even liked her, and the two events had been playing war games in her brain ever since. She pressed her fingers to a throbbing temple. And as if that weren't enough, there remained the small matter of Julia. Already she had phoned, twice, leaving messages to "call me, immediately."

With a heartfelt sigh, she smacked the file shut. There was a slim chance that Julia's urgency concerned wedding plans. Zane may have made those calls and firmed up a rehearsal time, although she had a bad feeling about that. His side of the wedding party had produced more headaches than Quade's mixed messages and several glasses of merlot combined.

The best man was stranded somewhere up north in his fishing boat, return time indefinite. The groomsman had chickenpox running rampant through his young family. Mitch had been asked to understudy if one or the other didn't make it, but no one knew when Mitch planned to show up, including their parents who had moved into his Sydney apartment to help care for their grandson.

Chantal buried her aching head in her hands. She needed to ring her sister. Unlike Zane's support team, she had vowed to be there for Julia. It was a sister thing, it was a bridesmaid thing. None of which made it any easier to pick up the phone. She dreaded Julia's inevitable questions, especially since she didn't have any answers.

What did I interrupt when I came out of the bathroom? What did he mean, he doesn't know if he likes you or not?

And wasn't that the million-dollar question! She shouldn't have stood there with her mouth flapping in the breeze while he walked away. She should have been mad as hell. She should have fired right back at him, some really cutting line like…like…

Well, same here, hotshot!

Except Chantal wasn't into self-delusion. In spite of all that had happened and not happened seven years ago, she liked him, she fancied him, she wanted him. Maybe her feelings were intricately linked with that early fascination, that whole first-teenage-crush factor, but there lurked a capacity for something infinitely more complex.

Did she want there to be an us?

Oh, yes. Absolutely. Indisputably. Unquestionably.

But—she drew herself up out of a slouch and lifted her chin—not unless he admitted to liking her. Not unless she believed he really did like her. Her pride demanded that much.

Pleased with such strong resolve, she blew out a breath, but it tickled the back of her throat and turned into a cough. And wasn't that the ultimate irony? After blaming her heated face on a fictional cold—to Quade and then to Julia—it looked as if she really might be coming down with one.

Checking the clock, she realized she had less than an hour until today's golf lesson and, with a gloomy sense of inevitability, she reached for the phone.

After five minutes of wedding updates and cross-examination—Chantal chose to plead ignorant on all charges—the ever-suspicious Julia caught a hint of the cold in her voice.

"Are you all right?" she asked. "You sound kinda croaky."

Concerned her nurturing sister might hotfoot it out from town bearing chicken soup and tissues, Chantal denied it, even while stymieing a cough. "Really, I'm fine,'' she lied as brightly as she could. ''And I'm on my way out. I'll talk to you later.''

''I hope this is leisure…?''

''It's golf.''

Julia sighed. ''Take it easy, okay? It really is supposed to be a relaxing way to spend a Sunday afternoon.''

Grimacing and trying not to cough, Chantal replaced the receiver, and all the way around the nine holes she played with Craig she really did try to relax. It proved impossible. In fact, the whole golf concept was proving nigh impossible, and that did nothing to improve her mood.

After returning home feeling miserable and sorry for herself, she wallowed in a herbal-scented bath until her skin turned wrinkly. Then she decided to allow herself another rare and luxurious treat…a night off.

Preparations were simple: she donned her comfiest pajamas and fluffy slippers, took the phone off the hook, and selected some soothing R & B for the stereo and something escapist from her bookshelf.

Just before she settled into the nest of pillows she'd created in front of the fire, she considered food.

Ice cream? Popcorn? Chocolate? One by one she rejected the options, and she couldn't lay all the blame on her budding cold. Lately none of her favorite junk food had interested her. As an appetite depressant, Quade was proving remarkably effective. Who knows, if he hung around long enough, she might even lose all the extra pounds she'd managed to accumulate over winter!

When the doorbell rang she was lost on the Hampshire moors, pursued by a brooding stranger with the cold hard eyes of a hunter. At the first chime, she closed her eyes. As the second chime sliced into her story-world mood of sensual menace, she swore softly but succinctly.

The word wasn't dang.

For the next six chimes she seriously considered ignoring her visitor. Except her car would be clearly visible in the open-fronted garage. And being—she checked the clock—after eight on a Sunday night, it could only be family. With the rest of them in Sydney, that meant Julia. Who she couldn't leave standing in the chill night air. No, really, she couldn't, although that didn't mean she had to welcome her with open arms. Perhaps if she described a bride whose red nose clashed horribly with her pink bouquet and whose vows came out as a hoarse croak…

Heartened by that plan, she bounded upright too quickly and needed to steady herself with a hand on the mantelpiece. Big-time woozy head, she thought as she tucked her open book under one arm and carefully stepped over the pile of pillows. And this time she couldn't blame Quade for the dizziness. A dozen more careful steps and she reevaluated that call.

The long narrow panels bordering her front door were glazed in an ornate frosty pattern that distorted size and shape, but not enough that she could ever mistake the long-legged, broad-shouldered silhouette as belonging to Julia.

Her most recent breath held in her lungs, expanding them until her chest hurt. She exhaled the backed up air in a long whoosh and realized she had stopped several yards shy of the door. She wasn't exactly dressed for company—had she even brushed her hair after her bath?—but Cameron Quade didn't strike her as the kind of man who would give up easily. As if to punctuate that thought, he leaned on her doorbell again. Hard.

She *was* home. If he stopped stamping his feet and leaning on the doorbell and rustling the paper sack in his hand, he would hear the soft strains of music drifting from beyond the very solid, very closed door.

So, why didn't she answer said door?

Scowling felt like a perfect response. Hell, he'd left a toasty warm fire, a Clint Eastwood restrospective, and a half-consumed bottle of his father's finest to venture over here. After Julia's concerned phone call he'd had no choice. Ten years in the cutthroat corporate world and he still had a conscience. His mother would be smiling down on that happenstance.

Beyond the decorative glass panels he detected movement and stopped fidgeting. "About bloody time," he muttered as the door swung open.

First thing he noticed was her put-upon expression. Then her crossed arms. Then her...*pink flannel pajamas?*

Yep, his eyes didn't deceive him. She wore pink flannel pajamas with some very lucky sheep gamboling across their hills and dales. And he'd been right about the music. It swirled from the living room at her back, as softly romantic as the flickering firelight and her pink cheeks and her ruffled curls. As his gaze climbed back to meet hers, he realized his sour temper had dissipated. Just from looking at her.

"You're alive," he said, purposely and perversely deepening his scowl. He didn't want to be wooed out of his dark mood. It suited him just fine.

"There was a doubt?"

"Your sister rang me. She was concerned about your phone being off the hook."

"That's because I didn't want to be disturbed," she said pointedly.

Quade chose to disregard her point and pushed past her. Ignoring the audible sound of her indrawn breath, he closed the door behind him. "Thanks. If you'd left me out there any longer I'd have frozen my... lemons...off."

Her eyes—which he noticed, belatedly, were glassy as well as bright and annoyed—seemed to finally take in his offerings. "You brought lemons?"

"And rum." He held up the bottle in his other hand. "Oh, and I remembered your CD."

"Thank you." The tight line of her lips softened. "I suppose Julia told you I'm getting a cold."

"Yeah. She wanted to come out here herself to administer TLC, but Zane was called out on a breakdown."

"And she's forbidden from driving alone at night." She sighed. "I guess it's a good thing, him being so protective."

"A very good thing."

She nodded, then lifted her chin. "Okay. You might as well get the I-told-you-so lecture over with."

"For playing golf in the rain?" Hell, he'd practiced that exact speech on his way down here but now she expected it, the idea suddenly lost its appeal. "I told you so," he said mildly, then, "What do you want me to do with these?"

A small smile curved her lips. "You brought them, so I assume you know what to do with them."

"My mother used to make some sort of hot lemon concoction. That's all I know."

Her smiling eyes widened. "Your mother gave you rum?"

"Hell, no. That's my contribution."

"It goes in the hot lemon drink?" She sounded dubious.

Quade shrugged. "Can't hurt."

Suddenly, unexpectedly, she laughed and the spontaneous sound danced all over his senses. "Oh, I think it would hurt."

"How's that?"

"I'm taking cold tablets which are making me woozy enough." She gestured at the rum. "I don't think *that* would go with."

She had a point but before he could agree he started thinking about her turning woozy and him having to pick her up and carry her to her bed, and he turned a little woozy himself. Which only annoyed him. Frowning, he shuffled the awkward bag into the crook of his elbow but it started to slip. They both made a grab for the spilling fruit, and their hands became all mixed up in a strange slow-motion juggling affair.

Their bodies bumped and brushed, hard planes against soft curves. Her laughter hitched on a breathless note, and he drew in air filled with a subtle green scent. They were standing close, and he wasn't thinking about germs. He was thinking about the fact that she wasn't wearing a bra under that soft giving fabric. He hadn't missed that not-so-small point.

"Ta-da!" She held the bag aloft triumphantly. "We didn't drop one."

Quade's fingers curled around the lone lemon in his hand. Lucky *she'd* been concentrating on the job at hand or they'd have been ankle-deep in fruit.

"Thank you for bringing these," she said. "It was really sweet of you."

Sweet? Obviously she didn't know what was going on in his mind. Not to mention his jeans. He shrugged. "I can't take the credit, although I had to improvise. Haven't a clue how to make chicken soup."

"Julia suggested you bring *soup?*" Her dark eyes narrowed. "She had no right!"

"She's your sister. That gives her the right to worry."

"But not to send you over here."

He shrugged. "You fed me last night."

"Oh boy, we're not back to who-owes-who are we, because I had about enough of that the last time." She huffed out a breath. "Okay, I'll accept your offerings because we are neighbors, after all. But then we call it quits. No more payback, no more mention of beholden. Okay?"

"Fine with me."

Their eyes met and held. And in that second something shifted between them, some tacit agreement made, a new bond formed. Neighbors? Quade rejected the notion out of hand. He didn't yet know what he wanted from Chantal Goodwin but it definitely wasn't neighborly sugar borrowing and back-fence chitchat.

"Good." She took the rum, then turned on her heel and headed toward the kitchen.

It would have been the perfect time for Quade to do something similar—to turn on *his* heel and get the hell out of there. But instead he found himself watching the sway of her backside inside those soft pink pajama pants and reliving the brush of her unfettered

breasts against his arm as they struggled to contain
those lemons.

He exhaled a long hot breath. Hell, he was one sick
puppy to be turned on by an obviously unwell
woman. In flannel pajamas. He forced himself to look
away, down, anywhere else, which is when he saw
the book lying on the floor.

Hunkering down to pick it up, he couldn't help but
notice the title. Chantal Goodwin read romance. Hot,
steamy romance by the look of the cover. He pulled
her CD from his jacket pocket and shook his head
ruefully. Romance novels and boy bands and the body
of a centerfold. Talk about contrasts and contradic-
tions—she was one surprise after another and every
new disclosure, each newly uncloaked facet, drew
him closer to capitulation.

Did he even want to fight it? Honestly?

Hell, if she hadn't looked so bright-eyed and fe-
verish he wouldn't be standing out here with a book
and a CD in his hands. Instead his hands would be
filled with soft flannel-covered curves, at least for as
long as it took to get those curves naked.

Did that mean he liked her? Because he had never,
not ever, wanted to get naked with a woman he didn't
like. Yes, he liked her. Probably had from the first
time she opened her sassy-talking mouth, or at least
from the first time she surprised him to laughter. But
he hadn't wanted to like her, hadn't wanted to open
himself to that possibility. It was so much easier to
classify her by stereotype: ambitious lawyer, Kristin-
clone, off limits. And until she tossed this cold, she
remained off limits. Pink flannel pajamas firmly buttoned. Centerfold curves covered. Which meant he

needed to get his sorry one-track mind out the door and down the road. Once he deposited her belongings.

With a new determination, he strode across the living room but pulled up short. Last night's straitjacket furniture had been shoved aside in a higgledy-piggledy fashion; a golf putter and several balls lay discarded in the middle of the floor; newspaper sections littered the coffee table. Hallelujah. He scanned further, to the fire crackling in the stone hearth, to the pillows spread before it. And it took less than a second for his imagination to paint a picture of her reclining there, sans pajamas, hair wildly mussed and creamy curves warmed by the dancing firelight. Desire, as quick and hot as those flames, licked through his body. He wanted his hands in her fire-bright hair. He wanted to spread her body before the flames. He wanted to make her burn.

''There you are.''

Quade shook his head firmly to clear the unruly heat, then turned slowly to find her in the kitchen doorway.

As her gaze swept the scene before her, her expression turned to dismay. ''You'll have to excuse the mess. I wasn't expecting anyone.''

''Why would I excuse it? I prefer it this way.''

''Oh.''

Obviously not the answer she'd expected. Now she looked nonplussed, more so when she noticed the book in his hand. Flushing prettily, she shifted her weight from one slippered foot to the other. Quade felt the banked heat within shift from lust to something softer, warmer. More dangerous. Damn. He should have left when he had the chance.

"I was reading," she explained, as if the book needed an explanation. "When you arrived."

He tossed book and CD on top of the mess. "Not working?"

Her chin came up a notch. "It's Sunday."

"Last Sunday you were working on your golf."

"Not after dark."

After dark. Two simple words that conjured up all sorts of images, most of them cast in red-gold fire-light. *Down puppy,* he scolded himself.

"I've put the kettle on. Would you like tea? Or coffee?"

"I should be going. Don't want to miss *Dirty Harry.*"

She looked interested. "Is it on TV tonight?"

"Yeah." He paused, not sure if he really wanted to know. "Don't tell me you're a *Dirty Harry* fan."

"Go ahead, punk. Make my day."

He didn't know if his overimaginative libido was playing tricks, but she didn't sound like she was quoting a movie line. She sounded…suggestive. The heat in his belly shifted again but he ignored it. He was leaving. Before he did something regrettable. Like making *his* day.

"Normally I'd say it's a classic and not to be missed." He tossed the lemon still in his hand and caught it. "But you need to be squeezing these into mother's magic remedy."

"You're not going to do that for me? What kind of neighbor are you?"

For an unseemly length of time, he lost himself in her smiling eyes. Then he saw the amusement dim, saw her nostrils flare slightly and, God help him, she moistened her lips with the tip of her very pink tongue. But the glassy brightness remained in her eyes and one corner of his mouth kicked up in a wry half smile. "I'm thinking, a pretty sick one."

"Oh my God." Eyes widening with concern, she slapped a hand over her lips but kept on talking through the splayed fingers. "Did I give you this bug? The other night…"

"When I kissed you?"

"Yes."

"Not that kind of sick." He shook his head. "I meant sick as in I'm looking at you in those pajamas and imagining taking them off you."

She must have inhaled sharply because her breasts rose, stretching the material of her pajama top…

He didn't mean to, he tried not to, but his gaze dropped to the top button. When had pink flannel turned into the world's most erotic material? *No, no, no.* Hands curled into fists, he started backing away. Toward the door. He was not thinking naked thoughts again, not even in terms of rubbing her chest with VapoRub. He didn't stop backing up until he reached the door.

Just to be extra sure he wrapped his hand around the doorknob before forcing his gaze back to hers. She was looking at him like *he* was the cot case. She had a point. For that reason alone he made damned sure his voice came out a lot stronger than his watery willpower. "Make yourself the hot drink, dose yourself up on those tablets, and take yourself off to bed. And don't get out again until you're better."

"But I have to—"

"Go to work? Really?" Dark eyes flashed and he knew he'd called it right. The thought ticked him off just enough to keep the words rolling. "Your idea of commitment to work got you sick in the first place, don't let it put you in hospital.''

''I'm not *that* sick. In fact I'm hardly—''

''What about next Saturday? Are you going to be fit for the wedding? Or do you want to give Julia something else to worry about?''

That tempting curve of mouth compressed in a tight line and remained silent. Satisfaction unfurled deep in Quade's gut—twice on the trot he'd managed to get the last word in. As he turned the knob and opened the door he decided to make sure.

''And ring your sister. Let her know you're all right.''

The Silhouette Reader Service™ — Here's how it works:

Accepting your 2 free books and gift places you under no obligation to buy anything. You may keep the books and gift and return the shipping statement marked "cancel." If you do not cancel, about a month later we'll send you 6 additional books and bill you just $3.57 each in the U.S., or $4.24 in Canada, plus 25¢ shipping and handling per book and applicable taxes if any.* That's the complete price and — compared to cover prices of $4.25 each in the U.S. and $4.99 each in Canada — it's quite a bargain! You may cancel at any time, but if you choose to continue, every month we'll send you 6 more books, which you may either purchase at the discount price or return to us and cancel your subscription.

*Terms and prices subject to change without notice. Sales tax applicable in N.Y. Canadian residents will be charged applicable provincial taxes and GST.

GET FREE BOOKS and a FREE GIFT WHEN YOU PLAY THE...

SLOT MACHINE GAME!

Just scratch off the silver box with a coin. Then check below to see the gifts you get!

YES! I have scratched off the silver box. Please send me the 2 free Silhouette Desire® books and gift for which I qualify. I understand I am under no obligation to purchase any books, as explained on the back of this card.

326 SDL DRRF

225 SDL DRRV
(S-D-01/03)

FIRST NAME

LAST NAME

ADDRESS

APT.#	CITY

STATE/PROV.	ZIP/POSTAL CODE

7	7	7
🍒	🍒	🍒
♣	♣	♣
🔔	🔔	🍒

Worth TWO FREE BOOKS plus a BONUS Mystery Gift!

Worth TWO FREE BOOKS!

Worth ONE FREE BOOK!

TRY AGAIN!

Visit us online at www.eHarlequin.com

DETACH AND MAIL CARD TODAY!

Seven

Ring *her sister?* For quite some time after Quade backed his way out her front door, Chantal felt like wringing her sister's neck!

Instead she wrung the juice out of too many lemons, all the while muttering to herself about pushy sisters and pushier neighbors. He had some hide coming into her house and throwing his weight around, no matter how splendidly proportioned his weight looked in tight jeans. Blinking that visual distraction aside, she sloshed her juice into a mug. Too much? Probably. She doubled up on honey to compensate.

Did he really think she needed reminding of her obligation to Julia and the wedding? Of course she would take time off work if she felt sick. She wasn't a fool or a martyr or a child...even if her taste in music and nightwear might point toward the latter.

Quade didn't seem to mind your choice of nightwear.

Frowning, she topped her mug up with boiling water. Or perhaps she had misinterpreted. Perhaps he'd wanted her out of her pajamas because they looked so hideous, which is precisely why she wanted to wring Julia's neck. For sending Quade over without any warning. For not having any chance to dress, to brush her hair, to glamify.

Leaning back against the bench she took her first tentative sip of his mother's magic remedy...and almost spat it back. Shuddering with distaste, she scraped her tingling tongue through her teeth. *Aaack.* Still, she mused, it was awfully sweet of him to bring the ingredients over even if he didn't stick around long enough to help her put them together.

Because he didn't trust himself not to touch her.

She shuddered again, this time with a hot/cold stream of sensual memory. No, she hadn't misinterpreted. Cameron Quade, acclaimed hunk, had confirmed that he wanted *her,* Chantal Goodwin, acclaimed man-deterrent!

The notion was dizzying, confidence boosting, and, quite possibly, the world's best cold remedy. Either that or the half mug of thick lemon glug she eventually forced down did the trick, because she woke the next morning feeling considerably more healthy. Her throat didn't hurt, her head didn't throb, but then she opened her curtains to gloomy gray dampness and decided to play safe. She could work from home; she had enough on hand to keep her busy.

Or so she thought before she spent the next forty-eight hours doing as much thumb-twiddling and phone-watching as concentrating on the contracts she was allegedly working on. When her phone only rang six times—work twice, Julia four times—disappointment hung over her with the same brooding presence as the rain clouds outside.

She had been so certain Quade would check up on her, if only to ensure she'd followed orders and stayed home. Perhaps he didn't care one way or the other. Perhaps he had only been responding to Julia's prompting, or acting on some sense of neighborly duty. Perhaps he had caught her cold, but worse, and he was really sick. And perhaps all the cold medication had scrambled her brain.

Wednesday she woke to a gorgeous spring morning, the kind where doubts dry as quickly as last night's dew in the sun's gathering warmth. Chantal caught herself humming as she dressed for work and laughed at herself. If getting out of the house felt this good, imagine how wonderful it would feel to do something really radical…such as ringing Quade to check if he was all right.

Hardly radical. He was her neighbor, after all. With no one looking out for him except an aunt and uncle whose existence centered around a whirlwind of business and social engagements.

Something radical such as…acting like a grown-up instead of a schoolgirl with a crush. She liked the man more than a little, she enjoyed his company, she definitely wanted to finish the kissing, so why wasn't she doing something about it? Why was she waiting around for him to make a move?

Because you don't know any moves.

In a moment of uncharacteristic ruthlessness, she stamped all over that voice of insecurity. Today she felt up for a challenge. Today she was going to do something scary, she decided, recklessly discarding her somber gray sweater and selecting a bright red shirt. With a dash of bravado she added matching lipstick and felt her pulse do a little red-lipstick salsa.

After work she would call on him, show him she was all recovered, let him know she wanted that ''us.'' And if *that* didn't qualify as scarily radical, she didn't know what did.

She followed the thumping of rock music to the shed behind his house and found him working on the MG...under it, actually. From where she stood she could see a pair of heavy work boots and a pair of denim-clad legs that extended far beyond the car's perimeter. They didn't need labeling for quick identification.

Probably that should have bothered her. Instead she found herself moving closer, skin tingling with the thrill of the illicit and unexpected. He hadn't heard her. She could look her fill. The impulse proved irresistible and she tracked those long muscular columns of denim slowly and thoroughly. For an indecent amount of time. All the way up to the top of his thighs.

A metallic clunk resounded from the car's underbelly, followed closely by a singular curse. Chantal started backward guiltily. He rolled a further foot clear of the car exposing his hips and several inches of scruffy black T-shirt. She was about to clear her throat, to say something to reveal her presence, when he must have reached up over his head.

That was the logical explanation for the shirt pulling clear of his low, hip-hugging waistband and exposing several inches of flat hard belly and a feathering of dark hair.

Oh my Lord.

Heat pooled deep in her stomach. Her breath came fast and shallow. Her skin grew hot just thinking about the possibilities of touching him on that bare slice of skin. With her lips.

Another clunk, several more pungent curses, and suddenly he slid all the way out. Hands still raised above his head, eyes fixed on her legs, he paused—but only for the scant second it took her to back up out of his space—then in one smooth fluid motion he was on his feet. Eyes cool, expression unperturbed, he reached for a rag and wiped his hands then turned off the blaring radio.

"Enjoying yourself?"

Chantal licked her dry lips, felt the caught-out heat in her face, but managed to match his conversational tone. "I had a nice view."

"Yeah?" His gaze rolled from the rag in his hands to her legs. "As nice as the one I copped from down there?"

Instinctively her hands flattened against the sides of her skirt—her remarkably proper straight gray skirt. "You couldn't see a thing."

"Hardly fair, is it?"

"I don't know about that. You *are* wearing jeans," she pointed out. "So, in all fairness, *I* didn't see a thing." She smiled. He didn't. He stared at her in a way that made her hold her breath, wondering what would come next, then he threw down the rag and studied his hands. "Been to work, I take it?"

Despite the casual tone of his question, she stiffened defensively. "Yes. I'm on my way home."

"This early?"

"The wedding rehearsal's tonight. In an hour, actually." And this was her chance to explain her presence, the reason for her visit. "When I hadn't seen you or heard from you, I thought I should check that you were all right. That you hadn't caught my cold or anything."

"I'm fine. And you're looking much better."

"Than the last time you saw me?" She thought about her nightwear and red eyes and laughed self-consciously. "That wouldn't be difficult."

This time he looked at her with lazy deliberation, a thorough once-over that made her think he saw beyond the practical skirt and bright but plain shirt to what lay beneath. Her skin warmed instantly, her senses sharpened.

"Nice shirt," he said softly. "And that skirt is a particular favorite of mine."

Because she'd been wearing it that first day? The day he'd looked at her and decided he was interested?

"But I do like you in pink flannel…and nothing else."

Of course. She'd been nattering about lemons and cold medication and her messy living room and he'd been checking out her lack of underwear. She tried—Lord, help her, she tried—but she couldn't rustle up anything but token umbrage. And heat. Lots of swirling, pleasurable, sultry heat. Especially when he started to close the gap between them with steady deliberation.

"Is concern for my health the only reason you came visiting?" he asked, stopping right in front of her. Chantal didn't even know she'd been backing away until she felt something solid at her backside. The car, she noted dimly. His hot, sexy sports car. "Or do you have another agenda?"

Did he expect an answer? With all of her erotic fantasies within touching and kissing and undressing distance? Then he planted his hands on the car hood, either side of her hips, and she felt a thready whimper building in her throat and a low thrum building in her blood.

"You're vibrating," he said.

And you're incredibly intuitive, knowing that.

His hand tugged at her waistband and she reached to help him. If Cameron Quade wanted her out of her skirt, who was she to quibble? He planted a cell phone in her hand, a *vibrating* cell phone, which she recalled, somewhat belatedly, attaching to her belt loop.

It was Julia—wasn't it always?—but at least her sister's introductory soliloquy gave her time to gather her scattered wits. As did the fact Quade had removed himself from her personal space. *Dang.* With a sinking sense of what might have been, she watched him redirect his focus to some piece of automotive paraphernalia on a nearby bench. To think he had almost been tinkering with *her* paraphernalia. She really would have to kill Julia this time.

One word, one name, drew her attention back to the phone.

"Quade isn't answering his phone?" she repeated. His tinkering hands stilled and he turned, met her gaze. *Julia,* she mouthed. "I suppose I could ask if he wants to speak to you."

She enjoyed the beat of a pause as Julia put the

pieces together. "Where are you?" her sister asked suspiciously.

"Right now? In his shed."

"Is he there?"

She waited for some signal, but he was leaning against the bench, expression deadpan.

"Yes. He's here."

She offered him the phone. If he didn't want to speak to her sister, he didn't have to take it. He took it. And when Julia's opening gambit delivered a quick smile to his face and her next line brought easy laughter to his lips, Chantal felt an intense stab of jealousy. *Whoa, there.*

Jealous of her sister? Her about-to-be-married deliriously-in-love sister?

Shaking her head at such irrationality, she glanced at Quade and saw him straighten out of his relaxed slouch against the car. A muscle flexed in his jaw.

"I don't think so," he said stiffly. "Isn't there someone—"

Julia must have interrupted...at length. He rubbed a hand over his face, issued a long defeated sigh. "All right. I'll do it."

Whatever Julia said drew a response that fell somewhere between a snort and a laugh. Then he looked up and met her watchful gaze, his expression so intense she couldn't breathe for a long eye-locked moment. "Lady, I'm holding you to that."

Holding her to what? Chantal's heart skipped a beat as she ran a quick inventory of the things she would like to be held to. His chest. That flat belly she'd caught a peek of earlier. One place she'd done more than peek at... And then she realized he'd been speaking to Julia. But looking right at her. What was that all about?

He finished the conversation with another short bark of laughter and, "See you later." Chantal had a pretty good idea why and when he'd be seeing Julia later and, recalling his initial reaction, she didn't like it.

"I thought you said you weren't doing anything that aggravated you," she said, taking back the phone.

"It's no big deal." He lifted a shoulder with seeming indifference, but she detected a tension in the gesture and in the set of his jaw. "It's just filling in tonight. Apparently Mitch hasn't arrived, Zane's out on a towing job, and Julia didn't know who else to ask."

Filling in at a wedding rehearsal, listening to vows and promises. Her heart dipped in sympathy. Damn Julia for putting him in this situation. And Mitch. "You don't have to do this. You could have said you were busy."

He was still leaning against the side of the car, legs crossed at the ankle, but he looked at her steadily, eyes glittering with some dark and dangerous purpose. "Who says I don't want to?"

"I thought—"

"I'm getting a free dinner, anything I care to drink. *And* a ride in a Mercedes coupe."

Is that what Julia proposed? What he was holding Julia to? It didn't matter that the arrangement was convenient and suited her just fine, it was the principle. This time she didn't have to summons indignation, it barreled on up, hot and ready for action. "Don't *I* have any say in this arrangement?"

"Only if it's quick. You're picking me up in thirty minutes and you might want to take a shower and change. I know I do."

"And what do you propose I change into?"

His eyes narrowed speculatively and the hint of a grin teased his lips. "Anything that's easy to get out of."

He made a sterling stand-in for Mitch at the rehearsal. Silent, tense, poker-faced. During dinner—a casual affair at the local pub bistro—he was uncharacteristically quiet, but then who could get a word in edgeways between Kree and Julia? Not to mention Bill the best man's interminable tales of his adventures up north.

Bill was sitting to Chantal's left and taking up far too much of the booth's bench seat with his sprawled posture and expansive arm gestures. This meant she'd been hemmed closer to Quade, on her other side, than was comfortable. Between Julia's smug glances and her acute awareness of his big hard body and the effort of participating in meaningful conversation, she felt ready to explode.

If Quade hadn't volunteered to chase up another round of drinks, she might well have done so. Reprieve. She blew out a relieved sigh and glanced toward the bar...and immediately tensed up again. Looking much more at ease than he had all evening, Quade leaned against the bar chatting with the pretty blond barmaid. As she watched, as she worried her lip and wondered if he'd been more uptight about the wedding vows or being jammed thigh to thigh with her, he threw back his head and laughed.

Longing rolled through her, so strong it winded her

for a long airless minute. She could only stare, bowled over by the intensity of the need, by the total power this attraction held over her. Then someone moved between them, blocking her view, and she managed to suck in a deep restorative breath. The someone she recognized as Prudence Ford, and she was sliding her considerable curves onto the bar stool right next to Quade.

Across the table Kree noticed, too, elbowing her brother and ordering him to, "Go rescue Quade. There's vultures on the prowl."

Suddenly it struck her that she had forgotten one important piece of information about Cameron Quade. He wasn't merely irresistible to *her;* he attracted women like steel chips to a magnet.

What could he possibly want with her?

Easy question for a smart girl like you, Chantal.

Hadn't he suggested she wear something easy to take off? She glanced down at her button-fly jeans and the shirt she'd buttoned tightly all the way to her throat. It didn't mean she hadn't considered wearing a pull-on skirt and pull-off top. Or that she hadn't left home with half her wardrobe discarded on her bed.

It simply meant she didn't want to appear too…compliant.

If he wanted easy then he could have Prudence Ford. That woman knew what she wanted from a man and went right after it. *Just like you vowed to do this morning, Chantal. Just like you would have done this afternoon, Chantal, in Quade's shed, against Quade's car, on Quade's car…*

What had changed between then and now?

Another no-brainer, if she cared to acknowledge the real thing that had been bugging her all evening.

If she cared to look beyond the hot, elemental desire to the plain, simple truth.

Standing in Julia's rose bower, watching the garden lights paint shadows across Quade's tense features, she had felt something grab hold deep inside. Not a simple pang of empathy for what he might be feeling, but something more personal. A need in herself that transcended desire, a need that spoke to her very core. She heard the breathy catch in Julia's voice as she practiced her vows, and she wanted that moment for herself. She wanted to hear those solemn vows of love and fidelity, of companionship and commitment. She wanted to gaze into lush green eyes and hear the words fall from her own tongue.

She wanted more than sex from Cameron Quade; she wanted it all.

There. She'd admitted it. She sat very still, forcing herself to *breathe in, breathe out, relax and calm,* freeing herself from the worst of the tension so that the warmth of the truth could settle over her in the way self-honesty usually did. It didn't.

Glancing toward the bar, she saw that Zane had completed his rescue mission and both men were returning to the table. Her confused dark gaze met his unreadable one, met and held, and her heart started hammering against her ribs. Her stomach churned.

She couldn't do this. She had to get out of here. Fast.

Pasting on a fake smile and not meeting anyone's eyes, she blabbered something about work tomorrow and having a lot to catch up on after her days off. Then she grabbed her bag and bolted for the door.

She had a good thirty seconds head start, more than enough time for a decent virtuous grievance to mix with Quade's simmering frustration. It was a volatile brew. By the time he saw her standing beside her car, her skin tone changing blue-green-white in cue with The Lion's flashing neon sign, a dozen alternate phrases clamored for first bite.

He was ten yards away and still tossing up between *you figured I'd walk home?* and *start unbuttoning that damned shirt, now!* when he saw her shoulders sag. His long strides slowed. His angry scowl cooled to a frown.

Then he cleared the long-tray truck that had partly blocked his view, and her sleek silver coupe came into sight. It had been keyed. From one end to the other, a deep ugly gouge. Every hot infuriated word fled his brain.

"Ouch," he said softly.

She didn't turn her head, but he heard her draw a fractured breath, saw the flash of anger in her eyes. "Not exactly the word I was thinking. In fact, not even close."

"I guess not." He knew not. "Had the same thing happen to my Beemer once. I'd only had it two weeks."

"I've had mine four." She touched the door, running her fingers gently along the wound. "What did you do?"

"Reported it and had it fixed."

She laughed, a short harsh sound completely at odds with the way her hand caressed her car, completely at odds with the softness of the night. "Then I guess that's what I'll do, too."

Straightening her shoulders, she reached for the

driver's door but he stopped her with a hand on her shoulder. "Give me the keys. I'll drive."

She shook her head. "No one drives this car but me."

"You're shaken up, you're angry, and you drive too fast when you're not. I'd rather not take my chances."

Her eyes flashed dark fire. "It's a nice night for a walk, Quade."

"Is that what you intended when you rushed out of the bar? That I should walk home?"

With his hand still on her shoulder, he felt her tension. "I...I wasn't thinking. I wouldn't have left you there."

"Pleased to hear it. Now give me the keys."

"I'm not angry anymore. And I'm a good driver."

"Subjective. I was in the passenger seat earlier. You drive too fast." She opened her mouth to protest and he didn't let her. "How about when you took on that truck up Quilty's Hill? You couldn't back off. Tell me, Chantal, is everything a contest with you? Do you tackle everything full throttle?"

His subtle emphasis on *everything* was deliberate. So was the way his gaze shifted to her lips, to the soft rise and fall of her breasts as she drew a shaky breath. The way his hand shifted on her shoulder, gentling, one caressing stroke down her upper arm and back to her shoulder. He felt her slight tremor, his own tightening response.

Then he took the keys from her lax hand and slipped between her and the driver's door. "And before you start thinking up reasons why I shouldn't drive, I don't speed, I do pay courtesies to other drivers and I sat on the one glass of wine all night."

Eight

After ten minutes, Chantal couldn't stand the silence any longer. She could have put some music on—God knows, she had enough to choose from—but she had already provided one opportunity for smirking without him seeing her entire boy band collection.

Besides, she didn't want him to think she was brooding over the who-drives issue. That would be petty, given she *had* been angry and shaken, and not only over the car vandalism. When she took off out of The Lion she hadn't outpaced the doubt demons—they had all come along for the ride. Better to talk than to brood, she concluded. Better for the sake of learning more about Quade, and better for the sake of quieting those demons and calming her jumpy nerves and distracting her jumpy imagination. *That* kept leaping ahead to the end of the drive.

Did he still want her out of these clothes?

Oh, dear Lord, she really had to stop thinking about that…

"I hope you don't mind me asking—"

"That phrase only ever precedes a question I *do* mind being asked," he interrupted, but she heard wry humor in his voice.

Good, she thought. *Humor is good.*

He made a carry-on gesture with one hand, a strong, capable hand with long, elegant fingers. He used them a lot when he talked and a lot when they were close. Recalling his hand on her shoulder, her arm, brought on a familiar rush of warmth. Imagining them on her bare skin caused a fiercer lick of desire, and then she felt him watching her, watching her watching his hand.

Caught, her face heated and she looked away, clearing her throat and remembering what she had meant to ask. "I've been wondering about your MG. Will you have it going soon?"

"Maybe." He smiled that sexy little smile, the one that just hinted at dimples. "Hope you're not thinking turnabout is fair play, because you are not getting behind the wheel of that baby. No way."

"Because I drive too fast?"

"Yes."

She didn't bother taking offence because she sensed there was more to come, *important* more to come. It was in the slight narrowing of his gaze, in the drumming of his fingers on the wheel.

"It's my father's car, really. He did all the early work, spent years chasing after parts. Ever heard the fourth rule of restoration?"

She shook her head. "Not that I recall."

"The bloke who has the part you desperately need got rid of it yesterday."

"Sounds like a cousin to Murphy's Law."

"Twice removed." Their eyes met and held for a moment, smiling, enjoying the subtle irony until he needed to look back at the road. "Dad lost his enthusiasm after Mum died and didn't ever get back to finishing it. It's giving me something to do while I'm waiting on Julia's garden plans. I decided to finish the job, for Dad. Kind of a..."

His voice trailed off and Chantal finished for him. *A memorial.* Wow. Overwhelmed by the notion, she didn't speak for several minutes, not until she could trust her voice.

"Is that why you're restoring the garden? Is that for your mother?"

His drumming fingers stilled. He glanced her way, surprise and something warmer in his expression. The something warmer took a firm hold on Chantal's heart, made her feel like she was smiling right there in her chest. "I guess I want things the same as they used to be, or close to. I don't know what that says about me...probably that I'm not much good at doing nothing."

"Or that you loved your parents and miss them."

He lifted a shoulder and shifted in his seat. Uncomfortably? Self-consciously? The band of warmth around Chantal's heart squeezed a little tighter. She was in big trouble here, she knew it, but she liked the feeling too much to fight it. Way too much.

"Any other plans for the way things were?" she asked.

"There's the land. It's been neglected, wasted. I've been thinking about what to do with it."

"You could start a free-range egg enterprise. You already have the stock."

He laughed. "If I could only find where they're hiding the eggs."

"Have you considered grapes?"

"They're on my short list. Why?" She saw a slight shift in his posture and felt a sharp shift in his interest.

"They do well around here. Climate and soil are ideal and there's boutique wineries springing up everywhere which add to the marketing options."

"Downside?"

"You have to know what you're doing."

"You sound like you do."

"Yeah, I *sound* like I do." She smiled wryly, thinking about how little she knew about other things, such as the getting-her-clothes-off thing. "I've done some work for the local Wine Producers Co-op, that's all."

"Are grapes profitable?"

"I couldn't say. James would know." When he lifted a brow in a *who's James?* look, she expounded. "James Harrier. He's a consultant who specializes in vines and orchards."

She offered to introduce them at the wedding, which changed the course of the conversation to Saturday's guest list and the fun job of seating such a motley assortment where they were likely to do the least damage during the reception dinner. Midway through the easy exchange they arrived in his yard, and he turned off the engine. Chantal had been aware of all that, but she kept batting the conversational ball back, knowing that once it went out of play she would have to deal with *what happens now?*

Now had arrived.

Closeted in the darkness, in the stillness, the atmosphere felt intensely intimate. She closed her eyes and breathed an intricate mix of man and machine, male and Mercedes. A night bird hoo-hooed and she heard the subtle creak of leather as he shifted in his seat, but he hadn't turned her way. His eyes weren't on her face, her body. She would have known.

Without opening her eyes, without so much as a peek, she could picture exactly how he looked, wrists crooked over the top of the steering wheel, a slight frown drawing his dark brows together as he searched the darkness of his garden for the owl. The image filled her mind, filled her senses.

"I haven't done this in a lot of years," he said softly.

"Sat in a car and talked?" Is that what he meant? She opened her eyes and turned to see him. *Exactly as she'd pictured.* "Did you used to do that a lot?"

"Not so much of the talking." Slowly his head rolled her way, and there was something about the smooth control of the movement, something about the white flash of his smile that mesmerized her. She could picture that exact motion in bed, dark hair against pale pillow, and the smile that seduced. "How about you?"

She swallowed. "Not me."

"You've never been parking?"

"No."

In a move as practiced and seductive as that smile, he turned his shoulders to rest an arm along the back of her seat. When his fingertips brushed her hair she ached to dip her head into the almost-caress. "Never necked?"

"No." She moistened her lips and watched his

eyes track the movement, felt those long, elegant fingers curl into her hair.

"No time like the present," he murmured, leaning forward slowly—much too slowly—and pressing his lips to her forehead in a kiss so gentle she barely felt it. But when he trailed those heavenly lips all the way to her temple, he left behind a delicate thread of desire that seeped all the way into her soul.

He eased away and her soul sighed with disappointment. "Have we started yet?" she asked.

Smiling, he touched her bottom lip with his thumb. "Just about."

That thumb continued to tease her lips, the bottom and then the top, turning her weak with desire. To be kissed, to be touched in other places. Hot, breathless, she imagined that lazy stroke tracing the line of her throat, cruising over the swell of her breasts, pressing against her tightly aroused nipples.

With an impatient growl she grabbed at him, sinking her hands into the soft knit of his sweater, dragging him those last few inches until his lips were on hers, her mouth under his. A satisfied sound escaped her throat as she opened her mouth, inviting him, accepting him, and the kiss exploded. From restrained exploration to consuming passion in one little sound, in one beat of her heart, in one long unrestrained stroke of his tongue.

Inspired, she followed him, learned from him, dueled with him. When he retreated she took the lead, sinking into the hot cavern of his mouth, feeling the smooth edge of his teeth, sampling every flavor. Pleasure sang in her veins, pleasure and a rush of feminine power she had never experienced before.

When she paused for breath, the hands cupping her

face slid to her shoulders and his lips slid to her throat. The nuzzling warmth of his lips, the gentle bite on her earlobe, made her hum low in her throat.

"If this is necking," she breathed, "then I'm sorry I missed out."

He laughed, a soft harsh sound, velvet in the darkness. "If you wore straitjacket shirts like this, I'm not surprised you missed out."

"I don't think I can blame my clothes." Her voice sounded thick and throaty, but then his hands were on her shirt, swiftly and expertly popping buttons.

"No?"

The backs of his fingers touched bare flesh, and she sucked in a shallow breath. "You remember me as a teenager. I was a natural born man-deterrent."

His hands stilled, she prayed because he'd finished with the buttons, not because she'd sounded too derisive or, worse, self-pitying.

"I remember you being a pain in the ass. I guess that's a deterrent."

Relief washed through her, so intense and heady she laughed out loud. "Yeah, well, I overplayed every hand trying to get your attention. The completely inept virgin with a king-size crush, that was me."

The ensuing silence reverberated through Chantal's body. Relief turned to cold dread. The big V word, proven atmosphere chiller, and she had just tossed it out there. *Dumb move, Chantal, very dumb.* She couldn't look at him, couldn't do anything but shake her head and cringe deep inside as he drew back into his own space, as she waited for his response.

None was forthcoming. No jokey rejoinders, no stunned expression of disbelief. Chantal felt so twitchy, so tightly wired, she thought she would snap. Pasting some semblance of breeziness on her face, she waved a hand dismissively. With the other she, belatedly, drew the open sides of her shirt together. "And I guess that was way more information than the occasion demanded."

She felt his gaze on her face, heard him inhale, and the whistle of breath sounded unnaturally loud in the oppressive atmosphere. "Are you still…?"

"A virgin? Technically, no."

"You want to elaborate on that?"

No, she didn't *want* to elaborate but seeing as she had dug herself into this hole, she might as well bury herself. "There's not a lot to tell. One regrettably ordinary experience a long while ago and that's my sexual CV. Short and not so sweet. Big surprise, huh?"

He huffed out a breath. "You might say that…although that in itself is no surprise. You've been surprising me and confusing me on a regular basis from the minute I arrived home."

His admission twined itself through Chantal's intense sense of letdown, halting the downward spiral. It almost sounded like… She studied him closely in the darkness but could read nothing in his expression. "Is this a good thing?" she asked.

"Yes. No." He laughed shortly. "I came home to sort out my life. I don't want confusion, I don't need complications."

"Perhaps you should have thought of that before you started undoing buttons." Defiantly she met his gaze, daring him to take issue. But when his gaze dropped, a liquid slide down her bare throat, her breasts tightened reflexively. She clutched the sides of her shirt together.

"Sex doesn't have to be complicated," he said as his gaze rose to meet hers. "Not if both players know the score."

And wasn't that the rub? He knew exactly what he wanted and she…she had a mind overflowing with insecurities and a heart overflowing with foolish hopes. She also had her pride. Swallowing, she lifted her chin. "You think, just because I'm inexperienced, I don't know what this is about?"

"You tell me, Chantal. Look me in the eye and tell me this is only about getting naked. Tell me you're not hanging onto some teenage infatuation that's all tied up in hearts and flowers and walks down the aisle."

"You know my opinion on marriage," she said stiffly. "I thought it was pretty close to yours."

"That's not what I asked. Why have you been celibate for so long? What have you been holding out for?"

She could tell him the truth. *I haven't bothered because no one had made me feel it was worth my while. No one has ever made me feel the things you do.* Or she could bluff.

Chin high, she forced her gaze to his, to the sharp glitter of his eyes in the darkness. "Your ego's severely inflated if you think I was holding out for you, especially since I thought I'd never see you again."

"Still not an answer."

Damn him. "You want a yes or no answer? Okay, yes. I do want to get naked with you. Is that what you wanted to hear?"

"All I want to hear is the truth, Chantal."

"And how will you know when you're getting it?

As you've pointed out more than once, I'm a lawyer, one you can't even decide if you like.''

''Oh, I like you all right.'' His voice was low and rough, his gaze dark and dangerous. Nerves started jitterbugging in Chantal's stomach. ''This afternoon in my shed, I liked the hell out of the way you looked at me. Tonight at dinner, every time your thigh brushed against mine, I liked you a little better. And just now, with my tongue in your mouth, I was about ready to explode with liking you.''

Oh. Her nerves stopped dancing and settled as a sick heavy weight in the pit of her stomach. All those things, purely physical. He didn't like her, he wanted her. Naked. For sex. A one-night stand, or maybe not even a whole night. Wham-bam, see you later ma'am. She knew all about the last.

Could she accept that and nothing more? Remembering all she had felt earlier in Julia's garden? Knowing she was more than halfway in love with him? Worrying her bottom lip, she stared out into the night, but he saved her from answering. At least for now.

''It's your call, sweetheart, and your time frame. Once you've stopped biting that lip, you know where to find me.''

Ever since he'd come home, Quade's conscience had ridden him hard. Some days he figured it was his mother's influence ensuring he lived up to her standards. Other times it was guilt driven, remnants of the months spent chiding himself for not seeing what was going on before his own eyes, in his own home, in his own bedroom. All because he'd been too wrapped up in his career.

Conscience, a need to do the right thing, obligation—whatever the reason, he found himself dressed in a dinner suit and walking through the flower-covered arches into Zane and Julia's garden on Saturday afternoon. Zane had asked him to come early, to maybe play groomsman, if Mitch didn't show. Mitch had shown. Expression distant, eyes flat, he looked as though he'd rather be swimming with sharks.

Quade knew how he felt.

Edgy, hollow, conflicted. All the things *he* had felt during the rehearsal would be ten times worse this afternoon, and that was without the extra complication of the bride's little sister. As good as a virgin. With a seven-year-old crush on him. He blew out a hot breath. Those revelations still unsettled him, made his feet itch with the need to bolt. Now would be the perfect time, before the sprinkling of guests who'd already arrived for the nuptials noticed him.

Except bolting felt too much like cowardice, as if he couldn't handle whatever she might dish up to him next. Quade shook his head and expelled a self-mocking laugh. What could she possibly come up with to top Wednesday's gobsmackers?

Three minutes later she rushed out the back door and answered his question. Holy hell. He could only stare. *That* was a bridesmaid's dress? Wasn't there some rule about taking the attention away from the bride? He couldn't imagine there'd be an eye—a male one, at any rate—fixed anywhere but on those curves encased in lace the color of her kiss. Rich, luscious, rose-pink.

With her focus fixed on her brother, she didn't see him right off. Thank heavens for small mercies. He needed recovery time, tongue-recoil time, eyes-back-

in-head time. Still, he couldn't stop staring as she delivered a quick message to Mitch, fussing with his tie
in a way that made his own feel like a neck noose.
An affectionate smile curving her lips, she turned and
started back toward whence she had come.

He knew the instant she saw him. Less than five
yards away her hurrying strides faltered and her smile
faded. She blinked, one slow-motion slide of her
lashes, and then she was there, right in front of him,
lifting her chin and pushing back her shoulders and
drawing all his attention to the way she filled the bod-
ice of the killer dress.

Did it come with built-in underwear? Because he
sure couldn't see—and he *was* looking closely—how
she could fit anything between the stretchy lace fabric
and her skin. From the low dip of the neckline to the
top of her shapely knees it caressed every contour.

When she tugged at the neckline, he realized how
long he'd been staring, and where he'd been staring.
Not good. He knew that for a fact when he looked
up into her furious eyes. It seemed like a good time
to take a teasing approach. "Is that dress legal?"

"It shouldn't be," she replied darkly, and he realized her crossness wasn't directed at him but at the
dress.

Releasing muscles he didn't recall tensing, he
grinned. "Do I take it this wasn't your choice?"

"Kree and Julia outvoted me."

He made a mental note to buy them both a drink
or ten.

Then someone called her name from the back of
the house and she wrinkled her nose. "Duty calls."

"Chantal."

Halfway to leaving, she paused, looking back at

him over one smooth bare shoulder. "It's a killer dress. The only way I can imagine you looking better is out of it."

Her lips parted on a soft surprised "Oh," and his body quickened. How many times the past two nights had he recalled the feel of those plush lips under his, imagined their moist openmouthed kisses on his body? He rubbed a hand over his jaw, a hand that stopped stock still as his gaze fastened on her retreating rearview, on the way the killer dress cupped the round curves of her buttocks.

With a low groan, he bowed his head in supplication. It was going to be a long, torturous evening.

Nine

Six hours later he was still riveted by that dress…or by the woman wearing it, he acknowledged ruefully, as he led the other bridesmaid through a series of fancy steps on the dance floor. Kree wore the same dress but on her it was just a dress, not an instrument of torment.

At that moment Chantal swung by, laughing up at her sixth partner in the half hour since the band struck up the bridal waltz. Quade clenched his teeth. So, okay, he hated the fact he'd been counting. He didn't begrudge her the turn with her father or her brother or the best man, but he begrudged the hell out of every other man with his hands on her body.

"You could always cut in," Kree suggested.

Yeah, and he could always swallow his pride and go drag her outside, into his car, and all the way home to his bed. Except he'd told her she had to come to him, in her own time, once she had nothing but sex burning in the depths of those espresso dark eyes.

She came by again, hips moving seductively in time to the music, and he felt a snarl building in his throat. When her partner slid his hand from a proper shoulder height to mid-back, the snarl slid through his teeth.

Kree held up her hands and stepped out of his hold. "James is a good customer. Don't hurt him too badly."

"One inch lower and he loses his hand."

Eyes intent on the other couple, he pushed through the press of dancers, and when he heard her throaty laughter, when he saw her fingers tapping a beat on the man's shoulder, he hoped Kree's good customer *had* lowered his hand. Just so he could inflict bodily harm.

Such uncivilized possessiveness was alien but undeniable. Before he could tap the man's shoulder he had to unclench his fists; before he could say, "Excuse me, she's mine," he needed to release the rigid set of his jaw. Surprise flickered across her face as he took her into his arms, and he liked the fact *he'd* jolted *her* for a change. Even more, he liked the way she felt in his arms.

Intense satisfaction chased all the violence from his body. When she lifted her head to talk, he splayed his hand wider against her silken back and tucked her closer to his body. More times than not, when they talked, they argued. Tonight he didn't want to take that chance. For ten minutes everything narrowed to the feel of the woman in his arms, to the certainty that she would be his. Tonight.

He deflected two attempted cut-ins, maneuvered

them past two attempted conversations, and would have happily kept doing more of the same if the music hadn't stopped. The MC took the microphone to inform the guests that Mr. and Mrs. O'Sullivan were about to leave, and while Quade allowed Chantal to slip out of the traditional dance hold, he kept a firm hold of her hand. She didn't seem to mind, at least until Julia sought her out, and then she tugged free to fall into her sister's embrace.

While they talked and wiped tears from each other's faces, a weird feeling settled over him, a foreboding that only intensified when Julia stepped to the center of the crowd and raised her bouquet high. With dramatic flair she paused to scan the faces before sending it sailing in a high arc. He felt positively sick as he watched the flowers spiral through the air directly toward the woman at his side.

When the jostling intensified, he stepped hastily out of the fray. When he heard a high-pitched shriek of delight, he glanced up to see a tall redhead waving the spoils of victory above her head. And with a jolt of surprise he realized Chantal was still by his side, that despite her competitive nature, despite the bouquet being hers for the taking, she had stepped aside. All his misgivings faded.

"You want to dance?" he asked.

Gaze steady and resolute, she looked him right in the eye. "I'd rather go home."

Quade's pulse kicked hard. "Are you sure?"

"I know what I'm doing, Quade. I know what I want. Do you?"

He nodded, a short curt movement of his head, and grabbed her hand. He wanted her and he was sick of not having her. But when he tugged on her hand, she resisted, and he turned impatiently. "What?"

"The other night I scared you off with the virgin thing. I want to be sure that won't happen again, that you won't run screaming for the hills because I'm not what you expected."

"I don't doubt there'll be screaming." His gaze fastened on her lips and his body burned with sudden intense need. "But that'll be you."

Quade's instructions for the drive home were short. "No chitchat, no revelations, no thinking."

How dictatorial, Chantal thought, objections taking shape in her brain. But then he took her hand and rested it on his thigh and that took care of the objections and the thinking in one fell swoop. Total mental vacuum until she moved her hand, spreading her fingers over the finely woven fabric of his trousers and feeling the instant grab of tension in the hard muscle beneath.

Then her vacant mind filled with vivid sensual images. The cool caress of satin against her naked skin. The hot gleam of his eyes as he lowered himself to the bed. Those long lean muscles flexing as he lifted himself over her body. Uninhibited cries of pleasure.

Champagne bubbles fizzed through her veins with dizzying, intoxicating speed. No doubt he *could* make her scream. He could, quite probably, make her do anything his heart desired.

Except it's not his heart doing the desiring, Chantal.

Before she could prevent it, her own heart performed the swan dive it had perfected over the past few days, plunging to a new low whenever she

thought about the impossibility of her feelings for
Cameron Quade, soaring high with Julia's series of
pep talks.

"It's the male mantra, sis. No intimacy, no promises, no commitment. The thing is, they don't *know*
what they want, apart from sex. They need showing.
They need loving."

"And what if he doesn't want me for anything,
apart from sex?"

"Do you want to find that out? Or are you going
to hem and haw until it's too late and he's gone."

"You don't think he'll stay?"

"Not unless he has something to stay for."

Julia was right. Once he finished putting Merindee
back together, he would be gone. He might call himself an ex-lawyer but he was a man used to doing, a
man used to challenges. A man worth putting all her
insecurities and self-doubts on the line for, because,
deep in her soul, she sensed he was The One for her.
For even the slim possibility of love, he was worth
the chance of heartache.

His leg shifted infinitesimally, but it was enough to
jolt her back to the present, enough to send a tingle
of awareness skittering through her nerve endings,
enough to cause her fingers to tighten reflexively on
his thigh. Were all his muscles so taut, hard, hot?
Instantly she was assailed with visions—taut, hard,
hot visions—of sliding her hand higher. Moistening
her lips, she edged her fingers a bold centimeter only
to find them instantly imprisoned.

"Not a good idea, sweetheart. Not if you want to
make it home."

The impact of those words—and the implication
behind them—pulsed through her blood. If she tested

him, would he pull over to the side of the road? Would he push her back in the seat and take her there, with all the hot urgency she saw in his eyes?

Oh dear Lord.

Heat, white and incandescent, suffused her, tempted her, teased her. And then she thought about afterward, about the inevitable awkwardness, and about him dropping her off at her own doorstep, his needs assuaged. No. That wasn't how she wanted this night to end, not by a long shot.

Settling back in her seat, she vowed to behave herself, at least until they made it to a bedroom.

His bedroom. She was pleased by his choice, pleased and so nervous she felt perilously close to nausea, which explained why she'd excused herself and bolted for the bathroom.

Getting this far had been relatively easy. For the last half of the trip his hand had covered hers, and the slow stroke of his thumb over her wrist steadily escalated her level of awareness. When he'd turned into his drive he must have felt her jumpy reaction, because he lifted her hand and pressed a kiss into her palm, a kiss that calmed as much as it aroused.

Then he took her by the hand and led her into his house, all the way to his bedroom. Eyes closed, she concentrated on the little things that suddenly seemed so difficult, important little things such as walking and breathing. And when she heard the pad of her bare feet on the hardwood floor—such a smooth, cool contrast to the jagged, hot edges of her senses—she laughed out loud.

"What's so funny?" he asked, and she heard the frown in his voice.

"My shoes must be still in your car. I don't even remember taking them off."

"It's a start," he said shortly, pulling her through the door into his bedroom. "One less thing I have to take off you."

If he'd started taking the rest off her then and there, she would have been fine. But a muscle jumped in his jaw and he'd looked so tense, so hard and untouchable, she freaked. And bolted.

Splashing water on her face cooled and calmed her. It also smeared the eye makeup Kree had applied with a liberal hand. Obviously not waterproof. Fixing the damage took several more minutes and, thankfully, distracted her.

"Stop being a coward," she instructed her pallid reflection. "You've come this far, now get back out there."

Nerves still danced about in her stomach, but she kept her head high as she padded back to his room. On the threshold she came to an abrupt halt.

Bare from the waist up, he sat on the edge of the turned-down bed removing his shoes. Soft warm light poured from a bedside lamp, turning the satin sheets to a gleaming midnight pool. As he bent and pulled at the second shoe the light fell across the smooth, clean lines of his back, playing on the flex of muscle, shadowing the dips and hollows.

The longing to touch was so strong, the anticipation so keen, she couldn't stifle the sound that rose in her throat. He looked up, saw her standing there, went still.

"You need help with that dress?" he asked in a low, controlled voice.

She licked her dry lips. "Yes."

"Good." Again, that muscle jumped in his cheek. "Come over here."

Heart beating so hard she could hear each individual thud, she started toward him. She saw the flare of his nostrils, the slide of his Adam's apple as he swallowed, the unwavering intensity of his eyes on her, and everything else faded. He wanted her. That's all that mattered.

He took one of her hands and tugged her closer, right into the space between his spread knees, and before she could think more than *nice move,* he hooked his other arm around her hips and pressed his face to her belly. It was such an unexpected embrace, so incredibly sensual, that Chantal thought she might shatter with the intensity of her pleasure.

Closing her eyes, she laced her fingers through his hair and sucked in a surprised breath at its softness. She had never equated softness with this man.

"Nervous?" he asked.

"Not any more."

Through the unsubstantial dress she felt the touch of his lips, the hint of a smile, and her toes curled against the hardwood floor.

"I love this dress." His hands skimmed her hips, slid down the back of her thighs, came to rest on her stockinged legs. "But it has to go."

In one practiced motion he peeled it from her body.

"Much better," he murmured and when his lips touched bare skin, Chantal's knees all but gave way...would have given way but for the hands curled around her hips and holding her steady, holding her captive to the touch of his lips, the stroke of his tongue, and the soft sounds of approval he murmured low in his throat.

Suddenly he rolled backward pulling her with him. The move should have been smooth except he caught her unprepared and she fell clumsily, laughing in nervous reaction as he tumbled her onto the bed beside him.

"Sorry." With an apologetic grimace she removed her elbow from his stomach.

"I'm not complaining." He had come to rest with his large hands cupping her bare buttocks. "Another surprise."

Chantal felt the heat of a flush warming her throat. "I had to wear a thong on account of that dress."

"It drove me crazy wondering what you had on under it."

The slow sexy circle of his hands was driving *her* crazy. "Now you know," she whispered breathily.

"Now I know."

She expected the teasing to continue, expected him to transfer his attention to the strapless bra that barely covered her breasts, but those tormenting hands stilled as he looked deeply into her eyes and the mood shifted to something more solemn. As he eased closer, need shuddered through her, an aching need to press herself against him, soft to hard, curves to flat lean planes, but his hands moved to her hips, holding her at bay.

"Slowly," he murmured as he lowered his lips to hers. "We have all night."

He started out as if he intended that one kiss to last all night: a languid sharing of breath, lazy strokes of his tongue, a slow meandering journey of her mouth. Chantal tasted champagne and chocolate dessert, pleasure and passion, and when he drew her bottom lip into his mouth she looked right into his eyes and the kiss became as involved as their myriad hues of green and amber, as deep as the strength and tenderness she felt.

Palms tingling, she explored his back, sliding over the smooth planes, touching each nub of his spine, slowing in surprise at the softer skin beneath his arms. Every touch he mirrored—the brushing of fingertips, open-palmed caresses, sometimes giving, other times greedy. A frisson of fear immobilized her when he unsnapped her bra, when she felt the slough of his breath against her bared breasts, but with one awed word her nerves fell calm.

They learned each other's bodies in slow increments, encouraged by murmured words of praise and pleasure. With hands and mouth he discovered secret places—behind her ear, inside her wrists, the dip of her spine—that set her body adrift on a sea of sensual delight. How could he know to linger over such places? How could he know such a perfect touch? How could he not know that her breasts screamed for equal attention?

He knew.

He knew so well that at his first touch, a gently exquisite pressure to one tight nipple, she thought she might weep. When he cupped the fullness of each breast in his hands, when she felt the pressure of those work-roughened palms and his low rough sound of need, her nails dug into the flesh of his back. And when he took those breasts to his mouth, when she felt the moist stroke of his tongue and the gentle scrape of his teeth and the insistent tug of his lips, she cried out, a sharp needy call for more.

So much, too much, not enough.

He left her breasts to slide lower, hooking his fingers into the elastic of her skimpy pants and peeling them from her body. A restless fire licked through her blood. Then his hands were on her legs, rolling away each stocking before sliding up her thighs to spread her, to find her hot and wet and wanting.

Craving.

And, oh, those hands. They knew how to torment and to tantalize, how to turn her into a panting, quivering mass of need. But it wasn't enough. She wanted her hands on him. She wanted his body on hers, in hers. Naked. But he rolled out of reach of her questing hands and onto his feet in one fluid movement. Light and shadow rippled across his skin as he shed the rest of his clothes, as he unselfconsciously revealed a body that turned her weak with wanting and renewed nerves.

He was extremely big, he was extremely aroused, and he was going about the whole find-and-fit-protection process with a practiced ease that reminded her of their extremely divergent levels of experience. But before she could finish thinking *what am I doing here and what am I going to do with all that?* he was back at her side, kissing her, reassuring her, touching her. Finding supersensitive flesh with those magical fingers and circling, pressing, lingering. Blowing all her fears out the back of her head as a delicious pressure coiled low in her belly, as a restless pulse pounded through her blood.

"Please," she cried, catching at his hand, searching out his gaze and holding it steady with hers, forcing her voice to a strong, purposeful level. "I want you. Inside me. Before you touch me one more time."

Heat blazed in his eyes as he pulled her body under his, as he leaned down and pressed a slow, intoxicating kiss to her open mouth. He eased away a fraction and smiled. "I thought you'd never ask."

And while she was still absorbing the irresistible impact of that smile, she felt him between her legs, apology tightening his face and his voice as he eased into her body.

"Bear with me..." He stilled, whistled out a breath between his teeth. "You're so snug." He pressed forward again, restraint taut on his lips, his brow, in the tendons standing out on his neck. "So damned...tight."

Chantal couldn't bear the suspense, the restraint, the slowness any longer. "And perhaps you're just too damned big."

"Oh, man." He shook his head, once, one side to the other. Then he laughed, a strained guttural sound that cut short in the middle as he gazed down into her eyes. "You're really something."

"I am?"

Eyes fixed on hers he eased partway out and she felt a mild moment of panic. Digging her fingers into his back, she held him there, poised at the brink of her body.

"Do you happen to know what that something is?" she asked.

Slowly he pressed into her, a little deeper this time. Sweat broke out on his forehead when he stopped, waiting for her body to adjust. "I'm working on it."

"Not nearly quickly enough."

"I'm trying—" he spoke through gritted teeth "—to be considerate."

"And I totally appreciate the effort."

Smiling sweetly, she lifted her hips in silent invitation but still he held himself there, unmoving, unrelenting. A tremor quivered through his body, through the long sweat-dampened muscles of his back, through the bulging arms that held him clear of her body, through the passion-hazed turmoil in his eyes. And in that moment Chantal felt an overwhelming sense of rightness along with an incomprehensible rush of tenderness.

She lifted a trembling hand to cup his face, touched the pad of her thumb to his lips and whispered, ''Go ahead. Make my day.''

He swore. Succinctly. Fiercely. And then he let himself go, plunging into her body with an intensity that rocked her to her toes, once, twice, three times, penetrating so deeply, so completely, that she knew she would never be the same again.

Knew she never wanted to be the same again.

''This isn't the way I wanted it to be.''

The guttural depth of his voice, the burning intensity in his eyes, the heavy pulse of his body inside hers, all combined to fill Chantal with a primitive power, an elemental strength. Then he bent down and dragged her earlobe between his teeth and she felt as weak and helpless as a newborn kitten.

''I wanted slow and steady,'' he growled near her ear, retreating then filling her again with one smooth languid stroke. ''Control.''

He repeated the exercise as he repeated the words. Smooth. Steady. Control. It was exquisite. It was mind numbing. It was sheer, unadulterated torture. Chantal whimpered low in her throat as the pressure built to an unbearable intensity.

Then he reached between them, seeking, stroking, one expert thumb and one flashpoint of wildly spinning sensation that traveled so quickly and grabbed so ferociously she could barely breath. Wave after wave of delight shuddered through her body and she cried out long and loud as his strokes gathered momentum, no longer languid and smooth and controlled, just an ever escalating force that hammered at her senses until he buried himself with a shout that sounded something like triumph and something like desperation, a shout of release that echoed through the room and reverberated through her soul.

Ten

She was watching him. Quade knew it the instant he came awake, yet the notion didn't feel as intrusive as it should have done. Or perhaps he was simply too spent, too sated, to register any feelings.

"How long have you been awake?" he asked, eyes still closed against the morning sun's white brilliance.

"A while." The sheets rustled softly as she shifted position. "Do you always sleep so soundly?"

"No." *Never. At least not in the last several months.* Yet he had slept like the dead, on the flat of his back, limbs heedlessly sprawled, with a strange woman in his bed and beneath several of those sprawled limbs. *Strange? Only because her presence felt too familiar—that constituted strange.*

He lay there a moment longer, waiting for the *what-am-I-doing-here?* misgivings to rouse him from his perfectly relaxed state. When they didn't he rolled onto his side, opening his eyes a mere slit to find her less than a foot away, solemn eyes looking right into his.

The effect jolted him to full consciousness in one heartbeat. Like the first shot of morning caffeine, he thought, still mesmerized by those deep espresso eyes...or by the expression in them. Grave, yes, but intensely focused, as if he were the only thing worth her regard. Chest tight—not with the expected dread, but *good* tight—he lifted a hand and touched her cheek, touched skin so pale and fine it seemed almost translucent in the bright light.

"Good morning." Her voice rasped with more than an edge of huskiness. From overuse during those long night hours before sleep claimed them?

The thought made him smile. "Yeah, it is. Especially since you're still here."

"I did think about leaving, but—" She shrugged. "It seemed like too much trouble."

Because she could barely move? Damn. Remorse washed through him. He had tried for restraint, for consideration, but she tackled lovemaking like everything else. Full on, take no prisoners, last man standing.

Heat chased hard on the heels of remorse, but he tamped it with thoughts of her inexperience. All but a virgin. "You must be feeling a bit..."

"Exhausted? Awed? Wonderful?"

"I was going to say sore."

"That too, but in the nicest possible way. Muscles I haven't used and all that." Self-reproach must have shown on his face because she suddenly smiled and touched a gentle hand to his frown. "Hey, no need to feel bad. I'm tough."

"You're a marshmallow." He kissed the soft sweetness of her lips before she could voice an objection. And because he felt like it. "Which, before you take issue, isn't necessarily a bad thing."

"You think?"

He kissed her again.

"And now you're trying to distract me," she murmured, clearly distracted.

Quade laced his fingers into her wildly tumbled hair and reminded himself how this conversation started. With self-reproach for the reason her hair arrived at that state—through excessive wild tumbling. He shouldn't be kissing her. Shouldn't be thinking about starting all over again the way he should have started. Soft and gentle and tender. Long quiet lovemaking that whiled away the hours and left a body blissful and boneless.

With a mental grimace, he removed his hand from her hair and scrubbed it over his face. Boneless was not an apt word choice, not given his current ever hardening state. *He* needed distracting.

"You up for breakfast?"

"What do you have in mind?" she asked lazily, propping herself up on one elbow in a way that enticed the sheet to mould her curves more closely.

"The usual. Coffee. Toast." *You. On toast.*

"French toast? With lashings of maple syrup?"

"Not unless you know somewhere that does home delivery."

Laughing, she shook her head and a tiny pink flower drifted to rest on his pillow. Eyes narrowed, he leaned closer and plucked another from her curls.

"Kree sprinkled those through our hair for the

wedding. Apparently when I took them out in the bathroom last night, I missed a couple.''

''Is that what took you so long?''

When she paused a second, hesitant, Quade instinctively held his breath. He wasn't sure he was up for any more surprises. ''Actually I suffered a mild panic attack.''

No surprise there. As soon as he'd pulled her into his bedroom he'd seen the anxiety and uncertainty in her eyes, but he'd let her go, left her to take her time, even though... ''Back here I was having my own panic attack, not so mild.''

''Really?''

''I thought you might do a runner. Out the window and across the paddocks.''

''Would you have followed me? Would you have chased me across the paddocks?''

Awareness arced between them—he saw it in the teasing smile, in the slight flare of her nostrils—and like wildfire the scene filled his senses. Pumping legs and panting breath, the pale flash of her dress flitting in and out of view, the excitement as the distance between them closed, as his hands found her in the darkness. The clash of bodies, the sensation of falling, rolling over and over in the lush green grass. The knowledge of having her under the moon and the stars. Under him.

''Careful,'' he murmured, cautioning himself and cautioning her from responding to the images that burned in his eyes, to the heat he saw reflected in hers. ''Let's just back this up a few degrees.''

''Okay.'' She exhaled a hot breath that whispered over his bare arm. ''Back to where you panicked about me leaving—''

"You first. What frightened you?"

"Insecurities." Her gaze dropped from his and she laughed softly, in that self-derisive way she had. "Or insecurity. I'm never sure if that should be plural or singular, although last night, in your bathroom, it felt like a whole seething mass of the suckers for a minute or two."

The need to reach out, to comfort her, was powerful. Irresistible. He touched a finger to her shoulder, stroked it the long beautiful length of her bare arm. "You care to tell me what a stunning, sexy, sharp woman has to be insecure about?"

"Not if it makes me sound like a neurotic nutcase."

He smiled but his gaze remained serious. "You don't see yourself the way I described, do you?"

"I'm sharp. I'm a woman. And you seem to have the knack of making me feel sexy."

"And beautiful?"

She sighed. "Look, I know the sight of me doesn't scare children, but when I was growing up I was always the shy, chubby one. The brainiac. The one with her nose stuck in a book…and I'm not talking about the Bobbsey Twins."

"Steinbeck? Tolstoy? Dostoevsky?"

"If they were on the syllabus," she said matter-of-factly. "Schoolwork happened to be the one thing I did well at, so I immersed myself in it. It became a habit."

"Study?"

"Success." Eyes lowered, she paused. Moistened her lips. "I started avoiding things where I thought I might fail. Sport, parties, boys."

"And after one…" *What had she called it? For-*

gettable? Regrettable? "One experience, you started avoiding men?"

"Let's assume it was a spectacular *un*success and leave it at that, okay?"

Yeah, he could do that. He could press a kiss to her wry smile and make some teasing comment and go start on breakfast. Or he could act on the compulsion barreling around inside him, the need to expunge the bad memories from her eyes, to replace them with spectacular present experiences. What the hell...

With lightning speed, he rolled her onto her back and pinned her to the bed. "So, how did last night rate on your success-o-meter?"

"Off the scale."

A simple response, three little words, but her lack of guile, the absence of premeditation, the clear honesty in her eyes, blew Quade away. He felt like puffing his chest out, thumping it Tarzan-style, swinging from the ceiling. And he couldn't help repeating her words. "Off the scale, huh?" Couldn't stop grinning like some big loon who *would* beat his chest and swing from light fittings.

"I heard you'd be a master class," she said, smiling right back at him.

"You heard? From whom?"

"My lips are sealed."

"I have ways of unsealing them." He nuzzled her neck until she squirmed against his hold, the laughter gurgling against her lips. "You know I can make you talk. And moan. And beg."

When he slid lower he took the sheet with him, playing it over the lush swell of her breasts until the nipples hardened and darkened, until he heard the hot

rush of breath past her lips. Ducking his head he wet
one, then the other, with one gentle slide of his tongue
then he rocked back to inspect the results.

Glorious. The contrast of milk-pale flesh against
midnight-dark satin. The gleam of their kiss-
moistened tips, the flush of arousal pink in her skin,
her lips plump and soft and begging to be taken. He
obliged, losing himself in the deep dark complexity
of the kiss, then, as he lifted his head, in the deep
dark complexity of her eyes.

"Now you've gone and done it," she murmured.

"Not hardly." Not yet, but soon.

"You kiss me like that and, poof, my mind clears.
I can't even remember what you're trying to coax out
of me."

"Does it matter?"

"Probably not, but don't let that stop you." Her
sultry come-hither smile was about the sexiest thing
Quade had ever seen. The fact that it came dressed in
nothing but pale skin and framed in dark satin didn't
do it any harm either. "I'm rather enjoying the process."

"Settle in because this particular process takes a
while."

A wicked anticipation danced in her eyes. "I don't
have anywhere else to be."

"No golf lessons to run off to?" He touched the
soft curve of her belly with the backs of his fingers.

"Yes." The answer whistled through her teeth as
he dragged his fingers lower. "But you're making me
forget again."

"Should I feel flattered?"

"Only if it doesn't augment your ego. That's had
quite enough stroking this weekend."

Quade snorted. "No such thing as enough stroking. Not where a man's...ego...is concerned."

She rolled her eyes and warm laughter streamed through him. It struck him how much he was enjoying her, not just the feel of her under his hands, under his body, but the banter. The teasing. The laughter that no longer felt strange on his face.

"If you ask nicely I'll give you a few pointers later."

"Are we talking golf?" All wide-eyed innocence. "Because I do need a few pointers. It's my big debut on Friday."

"You don't sound very concerned." Not for a confessed success junkie who, last time he looked, had trouble even connecting with the ball.

"When Godfrey set the time last week I just about lost my lunch, but you're providing one heck of a displacement activity."

Well, hell. Quade's hand stilled. A displacement activity. Is that all this was to her? Frowning, he looked into her eyes and saw the teasing laughter dim. What was wrong with him? Five days before he'd been ready to run screaming for the hills—her words, pretty accurate—when she'd revealed her long-term crush on him. He'd feared she would place too much importance on this affair, that she was looking for more than short-term pleasure. And now he was getting bent out of shape about *her* calling it a displacement activity.

"Is something wrong?" she asked. "You've gone awfully quiet."

Shoving his qualms aside, he smiled slowly and found her again. "Just trying to remember what comes next."

"Or who…" she murmured on a serrated sigh of pleasure. *Short-term* pleasure, Quade reminded himself as he watched her eyes widen with delight. That's all this was about, for both of them.

Over the next four days they shared plenty of pleasure and Quade gave her many pointers. Some were even about golf. "And wasn't *that* a waste of time," he groused out loud, just for a change.

He'd been stewing in silence for—he glared at the clock on his shed wall—five hours now, and it was becoming old. So was pacing the walls of his shed, cursing at every tool that slipped from his fingers, and blaming the clock. Where the hell was she? Throwing aside his buffing cloth, he expelled a frustrated sigh and gave up all pretence of work.

One phone call, that's all he needed. *Hi, I'm fine. I haven't wrapped my missile of a car around a tree. Talk to you later.* How much trouble was that? Too much, obviously. At last count he'd left six messages, three on her cell phone, one on her home phone, one on her work phone, and, when those cold spears of accident dread jabbed through him, one on her parents' phone.

What more could he do except stew and grouse? Julia and Zane were honeymooning and Godfrey didn't have a clue. He knew that firsthand. He'd willingly subjected himself to a whole afternoon in his uncle's company, nine holes of well-oiled maneuvers and manipulations, more aimed at getting him on board at M.A.B. than at winning a round of golf, and all for her benefit.

Because at breakfast that morning she'd knocked over the milk jug *and* burned the toast. Oh, she'd covered with jokes about clumsiness, but he'd known it was nerves, edginess, because of the afternoon's golf appointment. And as soon as she'd waltzed out the door, all breezy smiles and fake bravado, he'd picked up the phone and weaseled an invitation to join them. He'd wanted to be there for her, to provide moral and coaching support, because it meant so much to her.

And what had she done? She hadn't even turned up.

Godfrey had shrugged his concerns aside. "She couldn't make it this afternoon. Left a message with my secretary. Some fire to put out and she had to rush off somewhere. Work first with Chantal, always. That's why she's such a valuable member of our firm."

Hardly news to Quade, except this last week... *No.* Jaw clenched he shoved that dangerous thought aside. This week she'd been coasting—straight nine to five, few after-hours calls. Slow weeks happened along from time to time and, fortuitously, he'd gotten to share this one with her.

Didn't mean she rushed home to be with him. Didn't mean she chose his company above extra night hours. Didn't mean a thing in the big scheme of things.

When she hadn't returned his first message by seven, his irritation over an ill-spent afternoon had grown claws of worry, anxiety, unease. The golf had seemed so important. Impressing Godfrey the be-all and end-all. Hell, she'd even practiced in the rain to fit herself for this afternoon. She wouldn't have just blown it off...would she? *I started avoiding things where I thought I might fail.* No, not Chantal. She wasn't a quitter. Not any more.

So, what had dragged her off in such a rush? What had kept her occupied all this time?

The phone rang while he was in the shower and he didn't even stop to grab a towel. When he heard her voice, nothing but a simple *hello,* relief stole his breath, his strength, his cool.

"Where the hell are you?" he ground between clenched teeth. "Why didn't you turn up for golf this afternoon?"

She paused, just long enough for him to picture the hint of a frown furrowing the pale skin of her forehead. "How did you know that?"

Her quiet question, his racing pulse, the water pooling around his feet, the tick of the old-fashioned clock—every damn thing grated against the fractured edges of his temper. "Because I was there, damn it. Where were you?"

"I'm in Sydney. It's a long story—"

"Then let's just stick to the short version."

"Fine." One second to the next, her voice had chilled twenty degrees. *That* grated as well. "Mitch had a child-care crisis. I'm helping him out."

"You flew to Sydney to *baby-sit?*"

"I flew to Sydney because my brother needed me."

"Sounds like your brother needs to get his act together."

"Really?" she asked, the sarcasm so heavy he could feel it dripping through the phone line. "That's funny because, of all people, I thought you might understand."

"What? Your need to skip out on something you were afraid you'd fail at?"

Silence followed, so thick he felt its presence like a physical thing, like a cold, solid wall of dread. What was he doing here? Scrubbing a hand over his face, he struggled to form some words of apology. Some explanation for the irrational clutch of fear that had carried him along, unthinking, on a reactive wave.

"Actually, I didn't mean you skipping out on your career. I meant you might understand what Mitch has been going through ever since his wife decided marriage and rearing a child was inconvenient to her career."

Her words hit him sidelong with the force of a sledgehammer. *How the hell did she know about Kristin, about her decision?* "What are you talking about?" he asked slowly.

"About Mitch, about broken hearts, about pain that rips you apart inside." She'd been talking about Mitch's wife, her choices, not Kristin. He felt the tension in his jaw give a fraction. "Look, I only rang to let you know my whereabouts because I thought you wanted to know. For some dumb reason I imagined I heard concern in your messages."

"You did."

"Oh."

He wanted to say more, to explain why he'd been on that damned golf course in the first place, but not over the phone. He'd handled this whole thing poorly—okay, disastrously—from the get-go, and he intended making it up to her grandly. Not over the phone, not with her hundreds of miles away. In person. Very much in person.

"When are you coming home?" he asked, feeling

in control for the first time all day. It was a sensation he welcomed with open arms.

"I'm here for the weekend, flying back Monday morning. I'll be going straight to work."

"Will you call in here after work, on your way home?" Eyes closed, he waited for her answer. Told himself it didn't matter because if she didn't call on him, he'd be down there in a flash, bashing on her door, demanding she hear him out.

"Okay."

"Okay," he repeated, feeling like a man who'd just earned a reprieve, a guilty man who didn't deserve one. "I'll see you then."

Three hours until she was due—*if* she finished work on time, *if* she didn't have hours to make up after leaving early Friday, *if* she didn't decide to make him sweat it out in penance—and he was as edgy as the feral chickens that skittered around his shed. Every time he rolled out from under the car he seemed to startle one into wild wing-flapping retreat. The way he'd been tossing tools around today, he didn't blame the birds.

With a wry shake of his head, he propelled himself back beneath the jacked-up vehicle. It was a way to pass the time. Plus he'd found extra incentive to get the car finished—sometime during the past week he'd learned that Chantal had a thing for it. Not an historical interest, not a mechanical curiosity, not even an aesthetic attraction for the low-slung, red classic.

She had a fantasy. A hot, sweaty, no-holds-barred sexual fantasy involving this car. In what context he didn't know, but he was up for finding out.

With a grin on his face, he returned some of his

attention to the job in hand, the rest to a sultry stream of car fantasies. When he heard the low thrum of an engine ten or so minutes later, he thought the fantasy thing was getting a little too real and shook his head clear.

The engine cut out and a car door slammed. Quade's heart slammed against his ribs. This was no figment of his imagination, although he couldn't help conjuring up a few reasons for her early arrival. As edgy as he, she couldn't wait for the end of the day. She had to see him now. She had to have him now.

As he rolled out from beneath the car, anticipation filled his body with fierce intensity. The explanations and apologies better not get too involved. She better be wearing a skirt. Because car finished or not, he was up for finding out all her car fantasies right now. Fully up.

By the time she came through the door he was on his feet and wiping the grime from his hands. Before he'd finished one finger, he could tell she was in no mood for fantasies...unless they involved extreme violence. Great big galloping qualms trampled all through him, but he smiled regardless. "Would it help if I explained that phone call?"

Eyes flashing dark fire, she came to a halt in front of him. "It would help if you *explained* what you were doing on that golf course with Godfrey on Friday."

Eleven

"Helping you out."

Chantal had trained hard at the school of cool and collected, but every lesson exploded in a blistering red mist when Quade shrugged and calmly offered that answer. Rage shimmered through her as she whipped the rag from his hands and threw it to the floor.

"By offering advice to Godfrey? By recommending he send clients to big-city firms? Is that how you were helping me out?" She didn't wait for his answer, barely gave him a chance to narrow his gaze before she lit into him again. "Because from where I'm standing it looks more like you're helping out one of your old buddies. Andrew McKinley. Name ring a bell?"

His head lifted a fraction, as if she had rocked him and that felt good. Incredibly, vindictively good.

"Well, of course you've heard the name. After all, you recommended him!"

"Godfrey asked my advice on a hypothetical situation, I gave it. You want to tell me why that's a problem?"

"Damn right I do. That was *my* client. *My* case!" Not a hypothetical, but Emily Warner. To her mortification tears blurred her vision and she had to look away, to gather herself, before she could continue. "You had no right to interfere."

"Now hang on a minute—"

"I will not hang on to anything a minute unless it's your neck!"

He stared at her a moment, a muscle working in his cheek. "Don't you think you should take this up with your boss?"

"I did. But my boss happens to have this hotshot international attorney—sorry, *ex*-attorney—for a nephew and when *he* gives advice, it's gospel."

"I called it as I saw it," he replied all cool, unperturbed logic.

Chantal felt her cool and logic slip another notch. "During a casual chat on a golf course? For crying out loud, you didn't even have all the facts!"

"I had enough to discern it's a complicated case, one worthy of an estate specialist. I offered that opinion, and I stand by it."

"You don't think I'm up to it, do you?" Eyes narrowed, she glared up at him. "Same old, same old."

"If you're referring to what happened at Barker Cowan, then you're way off beam. You were a second year student—"

"Who you didn't trust to do a simple job."

"Don't you think it's time you let that go?"

Until Quade came back into her life, she thought she had. But somehow he managed to dredge up every buried insecurity, every old doubt about her ability, even when the voice of logic told her to take another look. Exhaling heavily, she looked away, down, studied an oil stain on the concrete floor.

"It's only a case, Chantal," he said very softly.

Her head whipped up. "It's *only* the most important thing in my life. I've been working my butt off for weeks on this, night and day and weekends. It's the case I've been waiting for. The one that will make a difference."

"For your career prospects."

Not a question. A statement of fact, as cold and hard as the look in his eyes. He folded his arms across his chest and Chantal felt a sudden urge to shake her head. *No, no, no, no. That's not what I meant, at all. I have handled this all wrong. Don't shut me out.*

"Shouldn't this be about what's best for your client?" he asked.

"Yes. You're right." Absolutely right.

"Pleased we agree on something."

Silence settled, awkward and uncomfortable. So much had been said poorly, so much left unsaid, and Chantal searched for an opening, a chink in his impenetrable expression. "What else did you and Godfrey discuss?"

"Is that any of your business?"

The coolness in his eyes should have been a signal. *Don't go there, Chantal. Don't pursue this.* But she couldn't help herself. "If it's about my workplace, then, yes, it is my business."

"No, and here's some free advice." The set of his jaw hard and unyielding, he leaned forward as if to lend weight to his words. "Don't ever presume that I will discuss any business with you, your workplace or mine, just because we are sleeping together."

Staggered—by his icy tone, his uncompromising expression, but mostly by the message—she took a step back. He was cautioning her against using their relationship, against using *pillow talk?* To what ends? To gain some kind of privileged information?

A short burst of laughter rose inside her. The idea was ludicrous. She'd been scratching for a conversation starter and he'd turned it into…into a character judgment. And how little he thought of her. As the notion took hold, hurt swamped her, so powerful it forced her back another step.

"Don't worry your conscience over that happening." Her voice sounded as tight and brittle as she felt. As if one more knock would shatter her like fine china on the concrete floor. "We won't be sleeping together any more."

"Quitting, Chantal?"

Chin high, she glared back at him. "You're the expert, Quade. What do you think?"

"Meaning?"

"You seem to have managed your share of quitting lately. Your job, your engagement. Your whole life, pretty much."

The calm line of his mouth thinned. Well, good. Finally she had managed to make some impact. "You don't know anything about that."

"Oh, and I wonder why? Could it be because you haven't told me one damned thing about it? Because all you were prepared to share with me was your body?"

"I never promised you anything else."

But during the last idyllic week she had allowed her heart to hope, to dream of a future beyond the bedroom. She had even convinced herself that Friday night's phone call was born of concern for her well-being, and her soaring hopes had delivered her home on a cloud of blissful anticipation.

To Godfrey's bombshell. To *this* eye-opener.

The man she imagined herself in love with had no confidence in her capability as a lawyer and no respect for her ethical integrity.

Head high, she forced herself to hold it together, to contain the angsty pain that screamed for release. To twist her mouth into a tight little smile and respond to that final slap of reality. He had offered her nothing but his body.

"No, you didn't."

Pride kept her walking out of that shed, head high despite the tears misting her vision, praying that her movements didn't look as wooden and jerky as they felt. That same pride kept her going over the next weeks, filling the long days and nights with any tedious, mind-sapping work she could find. It kept her from spilling her heartache to Julia, and it kept her driving past Quade's driveway with her head held high, kept her from succumbing to the powerful urge to pull the wheel right and not stop until she was in his arms.

Pride did all that, but self-honesty forced her to accept one truth—he had been right about Andrew McKinley. To build the strongest possible case, to ensure the best chance of winning, Emily needed a man like Quade's estate specialist buddy on her team. Unfortunately Emily didn't see it quite the same way.

Even after they traveled to Sydney for a meeting, she stubbornly insisted they could do without an arrogant city wig.

Two weeks later they had reached an impasse. Chantal expelled a frustrated breath and buried her head in her hands just as a knock sounded on her office door.

"Everything all right?" Godfrey asked from the doorway.

"Nothing I can't handle."

"I don't doubt that for a minute, but sometimes it helps to talk it through."

"Do you have a free hour or ten?" she asked with a mocking smile.

"If you don't mind walking while you're talking then, yes, I do."

Friday afternoon, golf afternoon. Chantal sat back in her chair and chewed her lip. For the past three weeks and four days Quade's *quitting* allegation had plagued her conscience. When Mitch's phone call came—that solid-gold excuse to bail out of the golf engagement—she'd been one second away from calling Quade, begging him to come and hold her hand. She'd proven herself as a first-rate nine-carat coward, one step removed from a quitter.

This afternoon, right now, she could make it up to herself. She could do this golf thing. She *would* do it.

Slapping her palms down on the desk, she pushed to her feet. "I'm up for some walking and talking. Thank you, Godfrey."

I hope neither of us regrets it.

Thirty minutes later the first arrow of regret pierced her right through the heart. Quade. In the Country

Club car park. Hauling a golf bag from the trunk of his car.

Her instant response—an actual physical jolt that stiffened her limbs and tensed her muscles—brought her car to an abrupt halt. And she sat there hunched over the wheel, heart beating erratically, while her eyes ate him up. The long line of his back, the sun-brightened gleam of his hair, the square line of his jaw, the dark shadow of a frown as he lifted his head.

His whole body stilled, paused as if he sensed her watching, and in that second she swore her heart stopped beating. Then he swung around, a swift movement that brought his gaze directly to hers. She could not look away. The pull of that vivid green gaze was so forceful she could feel herself trapped in it, sucked forward by it, as if into a vortex.

Dimly she heard the honk of a horn and, with immense difficulty, she shook herself out of a moment as intense as any she had ever experienced. The horn sounded again, more urgently, and she realized that she was blocking the road. With an apologetic wave, she released her foot from the brake pedal and steered into a park, a regular spot, not one situated in the middle of the road.

By the time she turned off the engine and looked around Godfrey blocked her view, but she could see he was shaking Quade's hand and that two golf buggies sat side by side behind their parked cars. Tension curled in her stomach as—somewhat belatedly—the significance struck. No coincidence but a prearranged meeting. There were no other cars she recognized, no one else preparing to hit off.

Just Godfrey and Quade and she as the third.

* * *

Avoiding awkward conversation was as easy as hooking every drive into the rough, as simple as pretending utter concentration on every approach shot and putt. But after four holes Chantal despised her cowardly tactics. Wasn't this afternoon about proving something to herself? Hiding behind trees was not the way to go about bolstering her self-respect. Playing no-speaks with her neighbor, ditto.

The next time Godfrey strode away to take his shot, she set her shoulders, stiffened her spine and made an effort. "Zane tells me you've almost finished the MG."

"Almost." He was gazing off into the distance, as if he couldn't stand to look at her. Swallowing the bitter hurt of that thought, she forced herself to try again. Three chances. Three innocuous conversation starters. If he couldn't do better than one-word answers, the message would be clear.

"And the garden's coming along? Julia thinks it's going to look magnificent in a couple of years."

"It will be." Three words. Wonderful.

They both watched as Godfrey's approach shot popped up, bounced all the way across the green and plopped into a deep sand bunker on the far side. Talk about symbolic. Her heart had just executed the exact same deep fall.

"Have you decided what you're going to do with your acres? Because I didn't ever introduce you to the vineyard consultant. I promised to do that, at the wedding."

Perhaps her last-ditch attempt at conversation had sounded as frantic as she felt, because he finally looked at her. Right at her. Her heart raced as she gazed back into those tired, shadowed eyes. *Tired? Shadowed?* She swallowed and tried not to conjecture why.

"I managed to meet up with Harrier," he said slowly.

"You did?"

"Yeah. His number's in the book."

Of course it was. But she'd been incapable of such simple deduction. The way he'd been looking at her, the way her crazy heart and body and soul responded with a wild cry of hope. Oh dear Lord.

"He mentioned how I cut in on him at the wedding. When he was dancing with you." Their gazes met. Memories of that night blazed between them in a bolt of vivid blue heat, before he looked away. His mouth twisted wryly. "Lucky for me he doesn't hold a grudge."

When he strolled away to take his shot—Godfrey's ball had just burst from the bunker in a spray of sand and come to rest by the flag—she released a long whoosh of breath. Her pulse still hadn't settled, and as he hunkered down to line up his putt, she allowed herself a brief, silent *whoop* of cautious optimism. Then she noticed the way his chinos pulled across the muscles of his thighs, and unadulterated heat obliterated her tempered warm optimism.

Through the heat haze she watched him sink his putt. Three putts later she'd done the same, a decent result for her, and when Godfrey finished they walked to the next tee and started all over. Two holes later she found herself alone with Quade again, as they walked toward their second shots. Godfrey's drive had landed on the opposite side of the fairway.

"I didn't realize you still played," she said, just for something to say.

"Haven't in a long while. Until…" He stopped suddenly, waited for her to do the same, to turn and face him. "Godfrey's invited me to play every Friday since I came back. I figured I'd spend all afternoon fielding offers to work with him, so I kept knocking him back."

Heart knocking against her ribs, she met his gaze. "Until the day I went to Sydney."

"Yeah. Except I invited myself that day. I wanted to be there for you."

The sincerity of that quiet admission knocked the stuffing right out of Chantal.

"I wanted to tell you the day you came home. I didn't and I've regretted it ever since."

That's what he'd meant by helping her…and she hadn't even bothered to ask. "I wish I had known," she said, her voice barely a whisper.

"Would it have made any difference?"

Remembering her all-fire rage that day… "Probably not."

He nodded. Then, turned and started walking again. Somehow she coaxed her legs into doing the same.

"I guess we both have regrets from that day." She felt his interest, a stillness in his gaze as it rested on the side of her face, but she couldn't look up. All her focus concentrated on placing one foot in front of the other and not screwing up her apology. "In the heat of the moment I said things I wish I hadn't. Especially about quitting your job." *And your engagement.* "I'm sorry. Truly, deeply sorry."

Their walking slowed until they barely moved, until they stopped, although neither turned. And in that

long silence the air felt so taut Chantal swore she
heard it sing, high-pitched with the strain.

It was her phone.

As she automatically reached for it, he circled her
wrist in an iron-hard grip. "Don't answer it."

"Okay."

He released his breath in what sounded like relief.
"I didn't quit. I was fired."

Wow. Cautiously she turned toward him and the
movement drew his attention to his tight hold on her
wrist. Frowning, he eased his grip to a gentling caress,
as if he intended to smooth away any marks left by
his fingers. A myriad of sensations swirled through
Chantal. The fierce longing to wipe that frown away.
To kiss it away. Warmth as tenderhearted as the
marshmallow he'd proclaimed her, yet cloaked in a
fierce possessiveness. To fight every fight for him, to
right every wrong.

"Why would they fire you?" she asked, hackles
rising. "Have they no brains?"

"They had their reasons."

Breath held, she silently implored him to share
those reasons. Whether he chose to or not seemed
immensely significant, a sign of his willingness to in-
clude her in more of his life. And just when she didn't
believe she could stand the suspense any longer, her
phone rang again, a shrill intrusion that she reached
to shut off.

"Go ahead," he said shortly. "It might be important."

"Not as important as why you were…"

Her voice trailed off when she identified the caller.
Zane's mobile, which he rarely used. He'd started carrying one in case Julia needed him urgently. Her heart

constricted with a sudden irrational fear. Three weeks to go, but...

"Is it Julia?" she breathed into the phone. "What's happened?"

She heard three words—pain, bleeding, hospital—before everything faded in a paroxysm of fear.

Twelve

One look at her stricken face, and Quade had asked two questions: "Where to?" and "How fast?"

At Cliffton Base Hospital they learned that Julia was being prepped for a Caesarian delivery and despite all the reassurance—it's precautionary due to the placental bleeding, thirty-seven weeks isn't too early, the baby's being monitored and is fine—Chantal's face had turned an ashen shade of pale.

She clutched the coffee he'd just fetched between hands that shook more than a little. "You don't have to stay," she said. "Kree will be here any minute. And my parents. They should be on the five-forty plane."

"I'm not going anywhere."

She didn't argue—not that it would have made any difference. He was staying. He didn't want to analyze why, didn't want to think about the ramifications, he just knew he wasn't leaving her. Not while her hands still trembled so badly she couldn't put down her cup without slopping coffee on the side table. Not when her eyes pooled with tears as she fumbled about in her bag. When she started to mop ineffectually at the spill with a wad of tissues, Quade reached for her hand.

"Leave it," he said more gruffly than he'd intended.

She stilled, tensing beneath his touch, and he turned her hand over to link fingers, palm to palm. For a long while he said nothing, simply sitting and letting her absorb strength and comfort from his touch. Gradually he felt an easing in her tension, an acceptance of the solace he offered, and when she gently squeezed his fingers the instant explosion of emotion poleaxed him.

For another long while he didn't speak, couldn't speak past the tight constriction that spread from his gut through his chest to take a stranglehold on his throat.

"Thank you," she said quietly.

He didn't bother with *you're welcome,* same as she hadn't added *it means a lot to me.* Both were givens.

After another minute, she spoke again. "You can't have a good association with hospitals."

"Does anyone?"

"Not everyone has your history."

Her quiet observation and the degree of perception behind it stunned him all over again. So did his sudden compulsion to invite her into a past he'd always kept under lock and key. Even from Kristin…but then she hadn't been interested in his past. Only in what his present could do for her future.

''We must have visited Mum, I don't know, at least fifty times when she was in Sydney. *Undergoing treatment,* they called it, and I remember wondering how the word 'treat' could be associated with what she was going through.''

Gently, barely perceptibly, she increased the pressure of her palm against his. Comforting him, encouraging him. Offering the same kind of strength as he had offered her.

''The sensory things get me the most. The smell, the rattle of those carts they use, the way the nurses' shoes squeak on the floors. They trigger this reflex reaction…I guess it's fear.''

''Of the very worst kind.''

He knew she wasn't thinking only of his mother's death, but of her sister and her unborn baby. Her fear that all would not be well with them. This time he returned the pressure of her fingers twined in his, tightening his grip until their forearms came into contact, elbow to wrist, along the aligned arms of their chairs.

''Thank you.'' No more than a husky whisper of sound but he knew she was thanking him for sharing as well as for the comfort.

Countless times over the past weeks he had replayed her words from that day in his shed, the day she walked out on him. *You haven't told me one damned thing about it. All you were prepared to share with me was your body.* Until today he'd clutched stubbornly at some warped sense of righteousness, because he'd never promised anything else, because he hadn't believed he wanted anything else.

But the instant he saw her again, the truth had hit like a sucker punch. Recovering from that initial blow had taken some time; so had accepting the truth. He wanted more. He didn't know how much, but it had started back on the golf course with his *I was fired* admission. Then, in the aftermath of Zane's phone call, his need to look after her, to be there for her, crushed any lingering doubts.

Now he had shared a glimpse of himself but there was so much left unsaid. Yet he felt no urgency, no cause for panic. Sitting hand in hand, offering her comfort and drawing some back, he felt a sense of harmony, as if suddenly all the fragmented pieces of his life had fallen back into place.

Glancing around the maternity ward, taking in the worried tightness between her brows, he knew this wasn't the time or place for the whole of his story but he would offer part as a sign of intention. The rest would wait.

"They fired me because another firm secured confidential information." Before she could voice the protest he saw in her eyes—and that instant defense warmed him gut-deep—he shook his head. "They were justified. It came from me."

"I don't understand. How?"

"Kristin's boss enticed her to extract information. Pillow talk." He released a disgusted breath. "I didn't even realize what was going on."

"That's treachery. She was your fiancée." Outrage brought color to her pale cheeks, fire to her dark eyes.

"First and foremost, she was an attorney."

"And this is why you broke up." A quiet statement of fact, not a question, and Quade knew he needed to explain the full circumstances later but, for now, this would do.

"Yeah, and why I fired into you so unjustly."

"I'm not Kristin."

"I know that." He'd known it for a long time; he just hadn't been ready to admit it.

"I'm sorry." A wry smile quirked her mouth. "Not about you breaking up with that evil woman, but about losing your job. About losing the life you had."

For the first time he felt no bitterness, no sense of loss. "They did me a favor."

"Really?"

"I took up law for the wrong reasons. After Mum died, when Dad could barely look after himself, Godfrey found out about the scholarship to Melbourne Grammar. It didn't cover everything, not by a long shot, and for the next ten years he paid the bills Dad couldn't handle, right through school and university.

"I had to prove I was worth all that money. Law seemed the perfect choice—prestige and money— plus what better way to prove myself than doing better in my benefactor's career?"

"You won't ever go back to law?"

"No." He was absolutely certain, at total peace with that decision.

"What will you do?"

"I'm going to put vines in. I've been looking at a viticulture course, thinking about external study."

Smiling—hell, he'd missed that slice of sunshine— she turned a little in her seat, enough that he could see the teasing twinkle in her eyes. "Farmer Quade, huh?"

"I'll see how it fits." But already the notion was sitting as comfortably as the feel of her by his side, as warmly as the effect of that smile. Eyes fixed on her mouth, he started to lean toward her...

"Chantal. There you are. I thought I'd never get

here. Has twenty miles *ever* taken so long?'' Kree fell upon them in a rush of words and hugs and demands. ''Tell me I'm panicking for nothing. Zane left a message with Tina and it was *so* not helpful. Tell me she heard it wrong. Tell me it's all good.''

Quade let Chantal explain, settling back in his chair as they reassured each other. A half hour later the rest of the Goodwins rushed into the room—both parents, Mitch and his son—and before the tumult of their arrival settled, Zane arrived wearing hospital scrubs and a dazed expression. The noisy rabble sobered instantly, and in the long beat of silence Quade noted the gleam of tears in Zane's pale eyes, and then an inkling of a smile. Still dazed, but a smile nonetheless.

''A girl.'' His deep voice hitched with emotion and he scrubbed a hand across his eyes before he could continue. ''We have a baby girl.''

He was instantly enclosed in a huddle of high emotion, questions falling upon questions without any pause for answers. Finally he pulled clear and held up his hands. ''I need to get back there. I just wanted to let you all know they're both fine. Everything's fine.''

''When can we see her? Them?''

''Is she dark like Jules?''

''The baby's all right, isn't she?''

As the questions streamed around him, Quade felt the first pangs of disquiet. Until this moment he'd been too focused on Chantal's worry to even consider the baby's arrival. A real infant, newly pulled from her mother's womb. *Uh-uh.* He took several automatic steps backward. *He was not ready for this.* And with so many family members, Chantal no longer needed his shoulder. Superfluous. He would leave them to savor their intense relief, their joy, the euphoria of the moment. Birth. Such a stark contrast to his hospital experiences. Such a stark reminder of his only remaining regret from Kristin and Dallas.

As he headed for the car park, he felt the sharp prick of tears in the back of his throat.

For a glimmer of a moment Chantal caught the look in Quade's eyes. Fear? No, more than that. Pain. Was he remembering his mother? The loss of his family?

She tried to catch his eye, but he seemed too tightly focused on his own inner thoughts, his expression remote. Never had she felt such a bittersweet ache of need, never had she wanted to reach out more, but before she could act Mitch caught her up in a wild whooping hug that swung her off her feet.

Around and around she spun, while Joshua bounced and yelled encouragement and Mother shushed their exuberance with loud disapproval. Back on her feet, her head spun with giddiness and when she finally regained her bearings, she turned around, once, twice, searching each corner of the large waiting room. Her stomach hollowed out. He was gone.

Disappointment settled quickly and heavily but lifted with equal alacrity. Nothing could dampen her elation nor her conviction that this afternoon marked a sea change in their relationship.

Relationship.

Her heart gladdened as she silently repeated the word. He had stayed and he had shared so much more than his body—he had shared the stuff of his heart.

With a resolute smile, she vowed that before this night was over she would share the essence of hers.

Call it telepathy or call it love-blinkered confidence, Quade knew she was coming. He didn't bother fixing dinner or turning on the television and although he opened a bottle of red, it sat untouched on the coffee table as he paced the floor with an impatience he had never experienced before.

He swore he heard the sound of her engine before she turned off the main road. Impossible but tonight his senses felt so finely tuned he believed it. He opened the door before she knocked, but she showed no sign of surprise.

"We have to talk," she said with steadfast purpose. "Really talk."

Quade knew that. But talk involved mouths and once his gaze shifted from the dark intensity of her eyes to her soft pink lips, he decided the talking could wait.

He couldn't.

"We will," he promised, pulling her inside and shouldering the door shut in one blink of her long lashes. In the next he had her pushed up against the slab of wood with her hands trapped above her head. *Now* she looked surprised. Satisfaction gathered low in his gut. So did a month's load of frustrated abstinence. "After."

She started to smile and he was there before it formed, sinking into her with a hunger that drove her hard against the door. His hands slid the length of her arms, fingertips to armpits, releasing them to capture her breasts with the same urgent compulsion.

She matched his mood immediately. Hands hard in

his hair, holding him to her mouth, she arched her back and pressed the fullness of her breasts into his hands, driving him wild with the need to possess.

Here, now, take no prisoners.

A torrent of heat flooded his groin as his hands slid to her buttocks, lifting her from the floor and hard against him. Without pause, she hooked her legs high and rocked her hips in perfect synchronicity with his. Perfect but for excess clothing.

Wrenching his mouth from hers—two hands didn't seem sufficient, teeth might come in handy—he started to right that wrong. He pulled her shirt from her waistband and started on the buttons but she was quicker. Hands already at his waist, releasing his belt buckle, unzipping, freeing him with a sharp cry of triumph.

Quade sucked in a long tortured groan at the incredible softness of her hand, moving on him with mind-numbing tenderness, stroking him until the heat and need roared in his ears.

He had to be inside her. Now. Yesterday. Last week. Forever.

"Condom." He hissed in a breath as she rolled her thumb over the head of his erection. "Jeans pocket."

His hands were otherwise occupied, under her skirt, ripping down her pants, touching her moist center without preliminaries. Or enough preliminaries judging by her instant response. Her breathing grew harsh, her pleas raw and earthy, and he had to stop, to plant his hands on her hips and remind her about her interrupted task.

"Protection. *Now.*"

"I can't," she breathed with equal desperation, "seem to get it."

Teeth gritted, he endured her fumbling ministrations, the exquisite pleasure-pain of her hand on him, stretching and rolling until he was sure his head would explode. Either one of them, both of them, it didn't matter. And when she was done, he rasped out something that might have been a curse or a blessing or a promise as he plunged into her.

Holy hell. How he had missed this. The hot caress of her body, drawing him in, to plunge again and again. The silken heat of her skin beneath his hands, the taste of her mouth, her throat, her breasts. The sounds of their breathing, harsh and ragged in the thick silence; the dark words they whispered, encouraging the fervent need to possess and be possessed.

It should have felt like lust, pure and elemental, but in those last seconds, as his climax gathered power and his senses clamored with the need for release, he gazed into her eyes and knew he loved her with the same unstoppable power as their joining, with the same savage intensity as the thunder that roared through his body as he came.

It took long minutes to collect himself from the ceiling, to gradually sink back into the shattered remains of his body. To realize where they were. Standing, slumped against his front door. More than half-dressed. His arms seemed barely capable of supporting him as he eased back from her body, out of her body, and in that instant he understood the significance of her stillness. The slightly puzzled look on her face.

The condom had broken.

Thirteen

Knees weak and trembling, Chantal sank to the rim of his bath and buried her face in her hands. Unfortunately that didn't obliterate either his surgically bright bathroom light or the memory of what had just happened in his hallway.

In the aftermath of that wild coupling, he seemed to freeze as if too stunned for words, and, when he had finally spoken, Chantal wished he'd kept that one succinct four-letter oath to himself. And that she had kept her eyes averted. Then she wouldn't have seen the unguarded flash of anguish in his eyes, wouldn't have been reminded of that moment in the hospital when he'd backed away from her family's joy over a new baby.

Fear had glazed his eyes. Fear of the consequences of that torn condom, sheer terror at the thought of being permanently tied to her through an unplanned pregnancy. The knowledge banded around her chest, driving the zillion shards of her splintered heart deeper into her flesh.

What a stupid loveblind fool she had been. He didn't love her. How could she have misconstrued so badly?

Tonight hadn't been about building a relationship of any kind. It was about sexual chemistry and raw desire and a man missing out for too long. It was about doing it, hard and rough, against that man's front door. And the consequences had to be faced.

Mustering her pride, she pushed to her feet. So, okay, she could take charge here. She could supply the response a man in this situation wanted to hear, and perhaps she could even toss in a cool, accepting shrug. She could do all that and maybe even walk out the door with her head held high. If not, she would die trying.

The living area seemed gloomily dim after the brightness of the bathroom, and that pretty much described the mood as well as the lighting. Quade stood in front of the unlit fireplace, his posture as stiff and unyielding as the columns of brick at his back. His face looked even more forbidding.

A lesser woman might have turned tail and fled, but, after one faltering step, Chantal pushed back her shoulders and kept on going. It didn't matter if it felt as though she were wading through treacle, all that mattered was getting through the next five minutes so she *could* turn tail and flee.

"Now we really *do* need to talk," she said with fake breeziness. "And it would be easier if you weren't glowering at me."

Hands on hips, he stared back at her. "You think I should be smiling? You think *you* should be smiling? Have you forgotten what just happened out here? Hell, Chantal, you might be pregnant."

"I don't think even yours would swim that fast."

"Now isn't the time for cute," he ground out. "Think about this."

"I have."

"Obviously not hard enough. I assume you wouldn't want a baby?"

Obviously *he* didn't, but what about her? How would she feel to be carrying Quade's baby, to be building a bond through their joint love of a child? How would she feel to see her man reduced to unashamed tears by the birth of his child? Hope bloomed, shy and tentative, in the remains of her shattered heart.

"It's not something I've considered," she said carefully. "At the moment I'm flat out keeping up with my job and my family."

"And if you are pregnant?"

The harsh intensity of his eyes sent a chill through her whole body, freezing out that first fragile inkling of warmth. And that just made her mad.

She didn't want to feel cold and hollow; she wanted to feel warm and whole again. In that moment it didn't matter that he didn't love her. He knew how to touch her, how to make her come alive, how to make her feel a thousand times stronger, a million times happier, than anything else in her life. She wouldn't let him cut her out of that. She would not allow that.

"Damn, Quade, I don't have to be pregnant. Isn't this what the morning after pill is for?"

His head rocked back as if he'd been slapped, and for a split second Chantal thought she had made a terrible mistake. But before that thought had half-formed his expression turned stony.

"You'll see your doctor in the morning?" he asked in a cold, flat voice.

Yes. No. Please, give me some sign. A muscle flicked in his tight, shadowed jaw, and she couldn't stand it any longer. Couldn't keep up the pretence any longer. She had to get out of there.

"Chantal."

She stopped before she reached the door but didn't turn around.

"Let me know if you change your mind."

"Well?" Kree asked, lowering her scissors. The question could have been for Chantal herself, or for the other stylist at the next station.

Tina lowered her blow-dryer and inspected Chantal's head through seriously narrowed eyes. "Sexy, yet stylish."

"Precisely." Kree smiled with satisfaction. "Now, don't go letting it get so out of hand again, okay?"

Chantal agreed. It was easiest, and sometime in the past seven weeks that had become her motto. Whatever's easiest. Whatever got every concerned family member off her back. Whatever got her through the next long day and even longer night.

Kree finished brushing away the loose hair and whipped off the cape with a flourish. When a frown creased her mobile face, Chantal felt a lecture coming on. Rising from the chair, she checked her watch and winced. "I'm running late, again. What do I owe you?"

"Don't keep running till you drop, okay?"

"You sound so much like Julia, it's scary."

Laughing, Kree reached for a bottle from the shelf behind her and plonked it on the counter. "You want to try this product? Your hair seems awfully dry."

She'd said much the same before she started cutting. As she ran her fingers through its length she'd tutted about the coarse texture and Chantal's stomach had pitched. Lately she'd been reading up on expected changes during pregnancy and breastfeeding. Hair texture wasn't supposed to change until much later.

"You want?" Kree prompted.

"Okay." *I doubt it will help, but whatever's easiest.*

Kree punched cash register buttons, and, from somewhere to her right, Chantal heard a soft whistle of appreciation.

"Cool car." Tina was peering out the window into the main street. "Know anyone who drives an old red sports car?"

This time Chantal's stomach did more than pitch. It rolled like something on the high seas. Dimly she heard other voices, conjecture over who might own such a vehicle, while the certainty turned her inside out.

Quade was back. After six weeks on some work experience jaunt at a Hunter Valley vineyard. At least that's what she'd extrapolated about his whereabouts from the various tidbits she'd heard from Godfrey or Zane or Julia. No one knew very much but they all knew more than she.

Six weeks of no see, no hear, no contact. No

chance to tell him that her only trip to the doctor had
been to confirm the home pregnancy kit result.

"Hello? Earth calling Chantal?"

She snatched the credit card Kree was waving in
front of her nose and dropped it into her purse, then
she forced her legs to take her out the door, forced
her eyes to locate her car, forced her hands to open
the door. Twice she fumbled her keys before she got
them into the ignition, but once the engine kicked
over she drew several deep calming breaths and allowed the solid feel of the wheel in her hands and the
smooth hum of the engine to gradually center her.

*This is a good thing. Once I tell Quade, I can share
with Julia. I won't have to pretend I can't hold Bridie
through horror of her sicking on my clothes. I can
hold her without fear of my response signposting my
secret. I can relax and laugh and cry and shake with
trepidation over this incredible, amazing, terrifying
event. This tiny life growing inside me.*

The shadow of a smile skittered across her lips as
she reversed out of the car park. A complicated mix
of apprehension and relief and anticipation rolled
through her as she drove down Plenty's main street.
Her glance flicked left and right, pulse rocketing any
time she glimpsed a red car. Whether in town or at
home, she would find him now. She would end this
now.

On the outskirts of town she started to accelerate,
picking up speed as the houses gave way to farming
land. She didn't even see the truck until it was too
late. A flash of movement coming out of a lane to her
right, too fast to stop, too big to avoid.

The last thing she heard before it hit was her own
cry of distress at not finding Quade, at never having

the chance to tell him about their baby. To tell him
she loved him.

"Ready to go, man."

Zane patted the hood of the MG he'd just returned
from a last test and grinned, the relaxed easy grin of
a thoroughly contented man. Quade tried not to resent
that, even as he tried to think of another reason to
delay his departure. The thought of walking through
the front door—*that* front door—and into his empty
house filled him with a panicky kind of dread.

"You got time for a drink?" he asked, hoping the
question sounded casual rather than desperate.

"Yeah." Zane's grin returned. "I can tell you all
about Bridie."

*Yeah, and then you can go right ahead and stick a
dagger in my gut.* He shifted uncomfortably. "On
second thoughts, I'd better be getting home."

Laughing, Zane punched his arm. "Come on, man,
I was only joshing. We can talk about your baby instead."

Dagger. Not in his gut, but right through his heart.
Reflexively he took a step back, but Zane was in-
specting the MG. *That's* what he'd meant by baby.

"Hey, Zane." Bill stuck his head out of the work-
shop door. "Tow call. An accident out near Harmer's.
You want me to take it?"

"Yeah. Please."

Zane sighed. "Looks like we'll have to take a rain
check, unless you want to go pick up a six-pack and
bring it back here."

"Sounds like a plan."

The phone rang before they'd finished their first
beer. Still laughing at the story he'd been telling,

Zane picked it up. "Bill. What's up?" His smile died, instantly supplanted by tension. His gaze jumped to meet Quade's across the office desk.

"Who?" he asked before Zane had the receiver down. Already on his feet. Already knowing in his gut.

"Chantal."

Fear sliced through him, as sharp and quick as a steel blade. "How bad?"

"According to the other driver, not too, but Bill says her car's totaled. They've taken her to Cliffton Base."

Quade was already moving but Zane stopped him before he cleared the office door. "I'll drive."

He started to object, needing to be in control, needing to be there, with her, now. But then memories of *their* fight over who drove assailed him, and he felt the fine trembling in his hands, in his legs. In his heart.

He nodded once. "Just drive fast, okay."

Chantal heard the commotion, the sound of raised voices, demands and objections, about five seconds before Quade burst through the door into the examination cubicle where they'd parked her. For another five seconds he stood there staring at her, head to foot and back again, as if checking that she was all present and correct.

Dimly, she heard the clearing of a throat and realized a sister had followed him in—obviously the one he'd been remonstrating with outside. "Now, you've seen her," she said with studied patience, "how about you do as you promised and wait outside?"

Quade's gaze didn't leave hers. "I'm not going anywhere."

Chantal felt her heart skip a long beat, then start to pound. She wanted to smile, to reassure him she was fine, to tell him never to leave her again, but she couldn't manage anything for the thickness of tears in her throat.

"What is she doing here?" he asked, finally turning to fix the sister with that fierce glare. "Where's the doctor?"

"Dr. Lui has examined her. She's under observation."

"Because?"

"Because of the bump on her head." The sister smiled reassuringly. "She's fine, the baby's fine. In a few hours you'll be able to take them home."

The door swung shut noiselessly behind her and Chantal closed her eyes. She couldn't bear to see the confusion on his face, couldn't stand the thought of watching it turn to anger. Perhaps he would leave now, as noiselessly as the sister.

When she felt the first tears leaking from the corners of her eyes, she squeezed her lids more tightly shut hoping to contain them, concentrating so hard on staunching them she didn't hear his approach, didn't know he had hunkered down at her side until she felt the touch of his hand, wiping away her tears with a hand that shook. Then kissing them away.

With a long sniffling breath, she managed to ease the flood but not to stop it completely. Through the moist blur she could see his dark scowl, the shadows beneath his eyes, the tightness at the corners of his mouth. She kept her gaze fixed there, away from his eyes, avoiding what she didn't want to know.

"Thank God you're all right. When I heard about your accident…" He trailed off, shaking his head, and she couldn't bear it any longer. Her gaze slid to his, found it and couldn't let go. The sharp intensity of fear, the soft glitter of tears. Oh dear God. *Fear for her; tears for her.* An ache started in her chest, so deep and bittersweet with hope, she could barely breathe. And she had to explain. She had to tell him everything…

"I have to tell you…"

"I saw your car and…"

They both spoke at the same time, both stopped at the same time. Both drew a breath. Chantal's hitched in the middle when he picked up her hands and touched them to his lips.

"I've never been so afraid."

"Me, too. They said the restraints and the air bags stopped me being…" A shudder run through her. The memory, the sound, her fear. "I thought I wouldn't have the chance to tell you."

"About the baby?"

"Yes."

It was no more than a hiss of sound yet it seemed to slither through her, filling her with a new trepidation, an old apprehension. When she tried to pull her hands away, his grip tightened and that lent her strength. Determination.

"I was going to tell you. Today. I heard you were back and I was on my way home…" Her voice shook and she needed to stop. Tears built again, annoying her, frustrating her. She hated this fragility, hated this shakiness.

"That morning…" He paused, studying their joined hands. "Did you go to the doctor?"

"No."

"Too busy?"

She started to shake her head but stopped, flinching. She'd forgotten about the bump. "No. I couldn't. I didn't want to."

His grip on her hands tightened painfully and she looked away, didn't want to see his anger.

"Look, I know you don't want this—"

"What?"

Startled by his loud exclamation, she stared at him openmouthed.

"What makes you think I don't want a baby?"

"Here, the day Bridie was born, as soon as Zane mentioned the '*b*' word, you left with the hounds of hell at your heels."

He rocked back, the look on his face almost comically bewildered. "You thought that was because I have an aversion to babies?"

"What else was I to think?"

"Is that why you reacted as you did, said what you did, after the condom business?" His grip on her hands was almost painful. "Were you saying what you thought I *wanted* to hear?"

She nodded, gingerly in deference to her head, and heard him laugh. It sounded like a rough husky mixture of relief and self-derision. It sounded like a glimpse of heaven.

"Talk about misconstruing." He shook his head. "When I saw Zane, the look in his eyes… Hell, there's nothing I want more than babies. Children. Laughter. My home as it should be, like it was when I was a child."

He huffed out a breath full of emotion, anguish hope.

"When I learned what Kristin had done, when I found out that I'd not even had a choice about that child..."

"Kristin was pregnant?"

"Yes, but I didn't know. She didn't ever tell me. She just went and had an abortion and carried on as if she'd been to have a tooth out or something."

Oh dear Lord. This woman was some piece of work. If Chantal weren't trussed up on a hospital stretcher with a head that threatened to explode every time she moved it more than an inch, she would chase her down and do some serious damage.

"I found out after the blowup at work. When I confronted her about that, she tossed in the pregnancy story as well. A going-away present."

"Do you still love her?" Immediately the words left her mouth, she wished them back. "Forget I asked that. Don't answer."

"I don't love her. I don't know if I ever did." The simplicity of that statement blew her away. That and the look in his eyes as he lifted her hands and turned them over, as he pressed a kiss into each palm. "I don't remember ever feeling the way I do about you."

Good answer. No, great answer. "How is that?" she asked huskily, needing to hear the words.

"Like I never want to let you go. Like I can't think of living any way but with you by my side. As my friend, my lover, my wife." He kissed the tender skin on the inside of her wrist. "I love you, Chantal and I know this isn't the most romantic place and, hell, I'm not so good with romantic gestures."

Chantal thought he was doing just fine. Especially when he did the down-on-one-knee bit.

"Will you marry me?"

When the stupid choking tears started again, she couldn't do any more than sob out her answer. "Yes." And again in case he didn't hear the first time. "Yes. Yes. Yes." And when he gently kissed her, on her forehead, her cheeks, and finally her lips, she thought her heart would burst with love.

"Will you take me home?"

He laughed, a soft rough-edged sound that hummed over her senses with the same gentleness as his lips. "I'll go see."

"Wait." Her demand pulled him up short of the door. "Come back here."

"Bossy." But he was smiling as he came back to her. "You must be feeling better."

"You have a way with your kisses."

"The healing touch?"

"Apparently." She paused, studying him soberly. The man she loved, the man who would be her husband. Her lifelong lover. "There's something I haven't told you, yet."

"I don't know if I can take any more of your revelations."

"Oh, I think you want to hear this one."

He arced a brow.

"I love you, Cameron Quade. With all my heart. There's nothing I want to do more than be your wife and fill your home with babies."

He smiled as he ducked his head a little, and she thought she caught the glint of tears in his eyes. "Will they all be as bossy as you?" he asked.

"Most probably."

"Good." He nodded with satisfaction and turned on his heel. "I wouldn't have it any other way."

* * * * *

Silhouette®

Desire®

presents

DYNASTIES: THE BARONES

An extraordinary new miniseries featuring the powerful and wealthy Barones of Boston, an elite clan caught in a web of danger, deceit and...desire! Follow the Barones as they overcome a family curse, romantic scandal and corporate sabotage!

Coming this February, the second title of
Dynasties: The Barones.

Sleeping Beauty's Billionaire
by Caroline Cross

Passion flares when Colleen Barone rediscovers an old flame. But will her now-wealthy ex-beau risk his heart with the Barone beauty who broke it once before?

Available at your favorite retail outlet.

Silhouette®
Where love comes alive™

COMING NEXT MONTH

#1489 SLEEPING BEAUTY'S BILLIONAIRE—Caroline Cross
Dynasties: The Barones
Years ago, Colleen Barone's mother had pressured her into breaking up with Gavin O'Sullivan. Then Colleen saw her gorgeous former flame at a wedding, and realized the old chemistry was still there. But the world-famous hotel magnate seemed to think she only wanted him now that he was rich. Somehow, Colleen had to convince Gavin she truly loved him—mind, body and soul!

#1490 KISS ME, COWBOY!—Maureen Child
After a bitter divorce, the last thing sexy single dad Mike Fallon wanted was to get romantically involved again. But when feisty Nora Bailey seemed determined to lose her virginity—with the town Casanova, no less—Mike rushed to her rescue. He soon found himself drowning in Nora's baby blues, but she wanted a husband. And he wasn't husband material…or was he?

#1491 THAT BLACKHAWK BRIDE—Barbara McCauley
Secrets!
Three days before her wedding, debutante Clair Beauchamp learned from handsome investigator Jacob Carver that she was really a Blackhawk from Texas. Realizing her whole life, including her almost-marriage, was a lie, Clair asked Jacob to reunite her with her family. But the impromptu road trip led to the consummation of their passionate attraction, and soon Clair yearned to make their partnership permanent.

#1492 CHARMING THE PRINCE—Laura Wright
Time was running out; if Prince Maxim Thorne didn't find a bride, his father would find one for him. So Max set out to seduce the lovely Francesca Charming, certain his father would never agree to his marrying a commoner and would thus drop his marriage demand. But what started out as make-believe turned into undeniable passion…. Might marrying Francesca give Max the fairy-tale ending he hadn't known he wanted?

#1493 PLAIN JANE & THE HOTSHOT—Megan McKinney
Matched in Montana
Shy Joanna Lofton met charismatic smoke-jumping firefighter Nick Kramer while on a mountain retreat. Joanna worried she wasn't exciting enough for a man like Nick, but her fears proved unfounded, for the fires raging around them couldn't compare to the flame of attraction burning between them.

#1494 AT THE TYCOON'S COMMAND—Shawna Delacorte
When Kim Donaldson inherited a debt to Jared Stevens's family, she agreed to work as Jared's assistant for the summer. Despite a generations-old family feud, as Kim and Jared worked together, their relationship took a decidedly romantic turn. But could they put the past behind them before it tore them apart?

SDCNM0103